Kattie

"I want my child to have my name.

"I don't want him denied his birthright," Sam continued. "He's a Fletcher!"

Josie stared, startled at his insistence on wanting a child he'd never counted on. "Or she," she said lamely after a moment.

"Or she," Sam amended firmly. "I want our child to know a father's love. I'll make it worth your while," he added when she didn't speak.

"I won't marry for money," Josie said firmly.

"Then marry me because you love our child."

When Sam Fletcher didn't get his girl in *Finn's Twins!* (#1890), Anne McAllister simply had to find the right bride for him.... The result: *Fletcher's Baby!*

ANNE McALLISTER was born in California. She spent long lazy summers daydreaming on local beaches and studying surfers, swimmers and volleyball players in an effort to find the perfect hero. She finally did, not on the beach, but in a university library where she was working. She, her husband and their four children have since moved to the Midwest. She taught, copyedited, capped deodorant bottles and ghostwrote sermons before turning to her first love—writing romance fiction.

RITA-nominated author **Anne McAllister** writes with warmth and wit, creating heroines you'd love to meet, and heroes you'll fall in love with…instantly! Her books are fast, funny and emotional—you'll be hooked till the very last page!

ANNE McALLISTER

Fletcher's Baby!

Harlequin Books

TORONTO • NEW YORK • LONDON
AMSTERDAM • PARIS • SYDNEY • HAMBURG
STOCKHOLM • ATHENS • TOKYO • MILAN
MADRID • WARSAW • BUDAPEST • AUCKLAND

ISBN 0-373-11932-1

FLETCHER'S BABY!

First North American Publication 1998.

CHAPTER ONE

SAM FLETCHER was no stranger to jet lag.

He knew all about the gritty, bloodshot eyes, the general lethargy, the tendency to yawn at inopportune moments. But he'd never had it affect his hearing before.

"Hattie did *what?*" He stared at his mother, who had pounced on him the moment he opened his apartment door.

That in itself was odd. Amelia Fletcher lived in the same Upper East Side building as her son, Sam, but she made it a point never to impose. Imposing was bad manners. Amelia Fletcher had never been accused of bad manners in her life.

Yet here she was at—what was it?—one p.m. (three a.m. Tokyo time, which was what Sam was on)—standing in the foyer of his Fifth Avenue apartment with a list in her hand.

"The lawyer said he couldn't wait until you got back in the States to read the will," she told him. "And since I had power of attorney while you were gone, it was entirely legal to do so without you."

"Of course, but—" More than his hearing must be going. He knew his devoted, eccentric aunt Harriet had died last week, and, while he regretted being abroad and unable to come to her funeral, he didn't see what the will had to do with him.

"She left you everything," his mother said again.

That was what he thought he'd heard the first time. Sam gave a quick, sharp shake of his head. "*Every-*

thing? You mean the..." His voice died as he contemplated what exactly Hattie's "everything" might imply.

In case his contemplation missed something, his mother, consulting the list again, spelled it out for him. "The house—the inn, that is—and all the furnishings, including her Ming vases, her Tiffany glass, her entire collection of Stickley oak, her Grant Wood sketches and her Frank Lloyd Wright elevations." Her voice slowed slightly as she continued, "She also left you three cats: Clark Gable, Errol Flynn and Wallace Beery by name." She shot Sam an amused glance over the top of her glasses. "A dog called—"

"Humphrey Bogart," Sam said heavily at the same time his mother did. He propped himself against the wall and shook his head. It was only marginally funny.

Amelia kept smiling. "Just so." She glanced down at the list again. "A parakeet."

Sam sighed and sagged. "Fred Astaire."

"And," his mother finished with a flourish, "an unidentified object simply called Josephine Nolan."

Sam jerked upright. *"What?"*

At the vehemence of his response Amelia took a step back, then looked at the list and nodded. "It's the last item on the list the lawyer faxed me. Josephine Nolan." She dimpled slightly as her lips curved in amusement. "I've never heard of a Josephine Nolan. What do you suppose it is? A rabbit? A hamster? A turtle?"

Sam didn't think it was funny at all. He knew exactly what a Josephine Nolan was.

"What in the hell is Hattie doing leaving me a *woman?*"

* * *

Shakespeare was undoubtedly right. First they ought to kill all the lawyers. Starting with Herman Zupper, Hattie's faithful retainer.

"What do you mean he's gone on vacation?" Sam demanded when Zupper's secretary said her boss was unavailable.

"For a month," she said calmly. "He and his wife are in Germany for their fiftieth wedding anniversary. That's why he had to call and speak with your mother before he left."

Sam grunted. He rubbed a hand over his hair. It was too short to tug which was what he wanted to do. "It's absurd," he muttered. "What the hell would Hattie do a thing like that for?"

It wasn't that he didn't have enough on his plate. He was the sole director of Fletcher's Imports, one of the most exclusive businesses of its kind in the world. Places like Gumps and Neiman-Marcus would die to offer some of the goods he imported for sale. But having such goods didn't mean he sat on his laurels. On the contrary, he flew all over the world, seeking out treasures, negotiating multi-million dollar deals. He did not have time to drop everything to run a little bed and breakfast inn in Dubuque, Iowa!

"I assure you, everything is in top-notch condition," the secretary said, apparently under the illusion that he thought he was being saddled with a slum.

Sam grunted again. He knew Hattie's bed and breakfast was a profitable business. Housed in a twenty-odd-room late Victorian mansion situated on a bluff overlooking the town of Dubuque and the Mississippi River, it was a charming place. It had even become a sort of bolt-hole for him when the pressures in his life became too much. Hattie, a childless widow, had always welcomed him with open arms.

She welcomed the whole world with open arms, Sam recalled grimly. As successful as Hattie's inn, The Shields House, was commercially, it was also the site of the biggest collection of white elephants Sam had ever seen.

The cats were just one indication of her lamentable tendency to collect things other people tossed out. He supposed he ought to count himself fortunate that she hadn't had more than three cats when she died. And a dog. And a parakeet.

And Josie Nolan.

And that was another thing! He'd assumed that Hattie, having no children of her own, would leave everything to Josie, whom she loved as if she were her daughter. What the hell was she doing leaving *Josie* to him?

He cleared his throat. "What's that, um, business about, um, Josephine Nolan?" he asked the secretary now.

"Josephine Nolan?" The secretary sounded baffled.

"In the will," Sam explained, feeling foolish. "Hattie left me the cats and the dog and the bird—" he grimaced as he said the word, all too aware of its appropriateness "—and Josephine Nolan."

"I'm sorry, but I'm not conversant with the exact items in the bequest. I only know we ran the property through a title check. I could enquire, if you wish."

"Never mind. I'll do it." He hung up, sank back against the sofa and stared up at the ceiling.

His mother, thank heaven, had delivered her bombshell and departed. Amelia had never much liked messy situations, and the look on his face and the words out of his mouth when she'd mentioned Josie had not promised tranquility, so she'd brushed a kiss across his lips, waggled her fingers at him and headed for the door.

"I'll just see you when you're rested, dear," she'd said. "Don't worry. You know Hattie. It's probably just her idea of a little joke."

Some joke.

Josie Nolan.

Josie Nolan was Hattie's innkeeper. Long ago she had been one of Hattie's white elephants. As a teenage foster-child living nearby, she had spent so much time gazing longingly at Hattie and her husband, Walter's, big house, that Hattie had invited her in. A few weeks later she'd invited Josie to work for her. Eventually she'd supported Josie through college. When she'd graduated, Josie had come back to help Hattie out.

Sam had first met Josie when she was a big-eyed, dark-haired child of fifteen and he'd been a worldly man of twenty-two. He'd teased her and chatted with her and forgotten her the moment he'd gone away.

Of course he'd heard "Josie stories" from Hattie over the years, and he'd always pictured the big-eyed, dark-haired girl who'd blushed every time he'd looked at her. But he hadn't seen Josie again until last fall, when he'd used Hattie's as a bolt-hole to avoid having to be best man at his ex-fiancée's wedding.

He hadn't even recognized her. Of course, she still had big eyes and dark hair, but she'd developed curves and a bosom—and legs.

Sam had been astonished at the length of Josie Nolan's legs. He hadn't ever thought of himself as a leg man. Hell, he couldn't even remember Izzy's, his ex-fiancée's, legs!

He'd hardly been able to put Josie Nolan's out of his mind.

Only, he assured himself, because he was still edgy about having been dumped. He'd noticed her because he was noticing women. Trying to regain his equilibrium after Izzy had thrown him over.

He actually thought she'd been right to break the engagement. So he'd been nice about it. He'd even understood. He had only to look at Izzy to see how much more deeply she felt about Finn, the man she had since married, than she'd ever felt about him.

But being nice hadn't been easy. And "nice" had its limits. He couldn't have faced standing at the front of the church and watching her walk down the aisle to marry another man.

So he'd gone to Dubuque and had spent a week doing wiring, painting and wallpapering...and other things.

It was the "other things" he was concerned about now.

Had Josie told Hattie what had happened that last night?

Sam wished to hell someone would tell him.

Or maybe he didn't.

He remembered parts of it. If he shut his eyes, he could see again the tear-streaked face of Josie Nolan when she'd opened her door to his light knock. He shouldn't have been knocking at all. He should have shut his ears to her soft, muffled sobs back then rather than try to be a good Samaritan.

God knew he'd been in no shape to comfort someone else on a night he'd wanted only to be comforted himself. It had been the night Izzy and Finn were getting married. And though he was happy for Izzy, and knew she was marrying the right man, it didn't help to know he'd been the wrong one.

He'd retired to his room with a bottle of his dead uncle Walter's best Irish whiskey right after dinner, hoping perhaps that a little Irish companionship could make him forget.

Maybe the whiskey had sharpened his hearing. Or maybe the walls were thinner than he'd remembered. Or maybe his tolerance for tears had been at an all-time low. Whichever, he'd heard sounds that surprised him. He'd known Josie was waiting for her fiancé, Kurt, to come and take her out for her birthday. He'd seen her pacing the floor of the parlor, then standing on the porch and looking hopefully down the road. Hadn't the bastard ever shown up?

Sam hadn't known. Then.

But then he went and tapped on her door, to have it opened by Josie, in a robe and nightgown and a tear-streaked face. He should have turned and run. Instead, he'd sympathized. He'd smiled gently and said, "They say that misery loves company. Come have a drink with me."

And she never should have come.

He didn't remember a lot about what had happened after that.

There had been soft sounds and sad smiles and touches. He remembered vaguely tangling his fingers in her long dark hair. He remembered breathing deeply of the scent of cinnamon and shampoo that over the past week he'd come to associate so strongly with Josie. He remembered running his hands up the length of those very long, very smooth legs. Later, after another toast to lost fiancés and missing ones, there had been more touches and more kisses, and then he remembered—oh, God, yes, he remembered—those long legs wrapped around him.

And then...

He remembered waking up in the morning with a

splitting headache and his cellular phone ringing and his secretary Elinor telling him that Mr. Nakamura was flying in this afternoon to talk with him about that shipment of teak furniture he'd promised.

Hungover, numb, Sam had promised to be there.

Then he'd looked around to see if he'd dreamed the whole thing. Josie, of course, because she was the innkeeper and made breakfast for the guests, was gone.

She might never even have been there at all—except there were two dirty glasses on the table next to the fireplace. And when Sam had looked further, he'd found her panties tangled in the sheet at the bottom of the bed.

He'd packed his bags before he went downstairs. He'd known he had to talk to her. But he hadn't known what to say.

He'd found Hattie in the kitchen, but no Josie.

"Kurt called," Hattie had reported. "He wanted to see her this morning. Since he missed last night with her, I said, go ahead." She'd smiled. "She'll be sorry to have missed you."

Sam had doubted that very much.

She was probably regretting last night had ever happened. She'd certainly gone running back to Kurt the moment he'd called. Well, fine, Sam thought. It had saved him making an even bigger fool of himself as he babbled his apologies.

But only for seven months.

He'd have to make them now.

And he would have to sort out this nonsense of Hattie's, leaving the inn to him. Josie was the one who had made it the success that it was. She was the one who deserved it. Not Sam. He didn't want anything to do with it.

So, fine, he'd give it to her.

No, he couldn't, damn it. There would be tax problems. For him. For her. His cash flow might permit him to cope with them, but hers wouldn't. If he gave the inn to her, Josie wouldn't thank him. She wouldn't be able to afford to keep it.

Maybe, he thought, she wouldn't even want it. Maybe she was already married to Kurt.

Stuffy, irritating Kurt certainly wouldn't want it. He didn't want Josie to have anything to distract her from him.

Sam groaned again, trying to figure it all out. He was sure it would be completely straightforward and logical if he weren't so damned jet lagged. He was sure it would all make sense in the morning. Whenever morning was.

He was too tired to haul himself up off the sofa and go into the bedroom to sleep. He curled up where he was and folded a pillow over his head. His last conscious thought was a question he sent winging its way to whatever spot his great-aunt was holding down in the hereafter.

"Hattie," he muttered, "what the hell are you up to?"

He gave himself twenty-four hours to fly to Dubuque, sort out the business with the inn, come to some sort of deal with Josie about running it until he found a buyer, and get back to New York to meet with a group of Thai businessmen he couldn't afford to miss.

He would have preferred to wait until Herman Zupper was back and dump the problem of the inn on him. He would have preferred to handle the whole mess by mail or telephone or fax.

He would, in fact, have preferred not to inherit—or go—at all.

But he would go, because Hattie had been good to

him, because she'd always loved him and sheltered him and supported him even when—especially when—being the only son and heir to the Fletcher empire got to be too much for him.

He wished now he hadn't put her off back at Christmastime when she'd called and encouraged him to come for a visit. He'd been surprised to hear her voice on the phone that cold December afternoon. Hattie ordinarily sent him telegrams when she wanted to say something. But that time, uncharacteristically, she had called.

"You really ought to come, Sam," she'd said. But she hadn't been her normally abrupt self, and it had been easy to say no.

He'd told her he was busy. Really busy. It was only the truth: he had been.

But too busy to spend her last Christmas with her? No, not that busy. He could have taken a few days, brought Amelia, and spent Hattie's last Christmas with her.

He hadn't. Because of the situation with Josie.

It would have been awkward. Uncomfortable. Hell, she and Kurt were supposed to be getting married in December, right after he got his degree.

For all Sam knew, he might have had to go to *her* wedding and give *her* away!

No, thanks. So he had said no to Hattie's last request. He hadn't seen Hattie during the last months of her life.

It was too late for that now. But he'd go anyway because he loved her—and he owed her.

And Sam Fletcher always paid his debts.

"Yo, Sam." The white-haired old man sitting on the porch swing hailed Sam as soon as he got out of his rental car and headed up the walk that crossed the broad lawn in front of The Shields House bed and breakfast. "'Bout time you got here!"

"Hey, Benjamin." Sam grinned as he gave the old man a wave and quickened his pace. He took the porch steps two at a time, holding out his hand. "How've you been?"

The old man reached out and shook it, then sighed and slumped back against the swing. "Missin' Hattie, you want to know the truth," he said. He gave a shove against the porch with his foot and set the swing to rocking.

"Yes." Sam commiserated. He'd expected that. Benjamin Blocker owed Hattie a lot. Like Josie, he was one of Hattie's strays. Only not a waif, a man with a past.

Once upon a time Benjamin had worked for her husband on the towboat Walter had plied up and down the Mississippi, but he'd drunk too much to be reliable and got himself fired. He'd vowed to dry out and put himself in various programs to do so. None ever seemed to work, and he'd go off again. Periodically, though, he would show up on Walter's doorstep, have a meal and take off again.

Then, the year Walter died, Benjamin had showed up on the doorstep when Hattie was in the midst of a plumbing crisis. Benjamin knew about plumbing. He'd saved the day.

Hattie, in her gratitude, had said, "Why don't you stay around? There's lots of work to be done."

Sam had thought she was asking for trouble, and had cautioned her against it.

But Hattie had just shrugged. "Let him have a chance."

"You mean it?" Sam remembered the old man saying.

Hattie had nodded. "I could use a man around to help out."

Benjamin stayed. Being needed—really needed—did something that all the well-meaning programs he'd tried couldn't do. Benjamin grabbed the chance Hattie gave him with both hands and hung on for dear life. Sam didn't think he'd ever taken a drink again. He'd certainly never turned up drunk as far as Sam had ever heard. From then on, Benjamin kept the plumbing in perfect running order, installed whirlpool baths in four of the rooms, and definitely earned his keep.

Later that year, when Hattie bought a little house halfway down the bluff, intending to use it for long-term rentals, Benjamin had helped her restore it, then moved into the bottom floor as an on-site caretaker. A little over a year ago Hattie had deeded the house to him. He was taken care of.

Which was probably, Sam reflected, the only reason he hadn't got left Benjamin in the will.

Or Cletus, another of Hattie's "projects," who came ambling up the walk now. Cletus was perhaps seventy-five to Benjamin's eighty, and he, too, had been aimless when Hattie had met him at the soup kitchen. They'd talked about how nice the lilacs were that year, and Hattie had invited him up to see hers.

He'd arrived on a bicycle, looking a bit shabby but clean in a threadbare navy blazer and khakis, with a distinctive sprig of lilac in his buttonhole.

He thought hers needed pruning. "Have to do it in the fall," he'd told her. Then he'd surveyed the lawn and gardens critically. "Got to get wire props for those peonies,'' he had told her. ''And a better arbor for the grapes.''

''Can you make an arbor?'' Hattie had asked.

Cletus had made the arbor and had been here ever since.

Now he set the wheelbarrow full of potting plants down and stood looking Sam up and down.

''How you doing, Cletus?'' Sam offered his hand.

Cletus grunted and took Sam's hand, but the shake he gave it was little more than a jerk. ''Took you long enough.''

Sam frowned. ''I got here as soon as I could. I was in the Orient when Hattie died. I couldn't get back in time for the funeral.''

He got another grunt. Two in fact. One from each of them.

He frowned. ''I'm here now. Don't worry. Everything will be fine. I'll get things sorted out.''

Cletus looked stern. ''Damn right you will.''

''I'm sure you'll do the right thing.'' Benjamin gave Cletus a satisfied nod.

Sam was glad someone had faith in him. ''Of course I will,'' he said stoutly. He looked at Cletus to see how he'd taken Benjamin's support. The glance netted him an uncompromisingly steely stare.

''We're counting on you,'' Cletus said at last.

What the hell was going on here? Did they think he was going to sell the place out from under them?

''I'll see that you're both taken care of,'' he promised.

''Tain't us we're worried about,'' Cletus said. ''It's Josie.''

''I'll take care of Josie,'' Sam promised.

It was apparently the right thing to say. Both men beamed.

"Knew it," Benjamin said.

"Good lad," Cletus agreed, and clapped him on the back.

Sam allowed himself a moment to bask in their approval, then asked, "Where is she?"

"In the kitchen. She didn't say you were comin'."

Sam shifted from one foot to the other. "I didn't call." And he wasn't explaining why. But there was one thing he wanted to know before he saw her. "Is...she married?"

Benjamin stared at him. "Married?"

Cletus took off his spectacles and wiped them. Then, setting them back on his nose, he looked squarely at Sam. "Not yet."

Sam sighed. He supposed he shouldn't be surprised. He'd never had much appreciation for Kurt's finer qualities. He might be God's gift to deep thinkers everywhere, but he seemed entirely too cavalier about the woman he loved for Sam's taste.

"I'll go talk to her now." He started around the house toward the back door.

He could have gone to the front, but that would have meant ringing the bell and waiting for Josie to let him in. It would have meant she could see him before she opened the double leaded glass doors. The advantage would have been hers.

He wanted the advantage to be his.

He saw her through the kitchen window. There was a long island counter just inside the door and she was behind it, arranging flowers. Josie was tall, a good four inches taller than Izzy, with long, lush brown hair that had always glinted red in the sun. Sam remembered wanting to run his fingers through her hair from the first day he'd met her when she was barely more than a child. He'd always restrained himself until—

He jammed his hands in his pockets.

She could have seen him coming if she'd been looking up. But she was concentrating on putting flowers in a variety of vases. Daffodils, baby's breath, carnations— bright fresh bouquets that brought the outdoors into each room, as she'd once told him. Sam remembered the drill.

She'd been doing it the day of her birthday, the day Kurt had stood her up, the day he'd invited her to his room for a drink, the day—

Hell! The only thing now was to apologize, admit he'd made a mistake—that they'd *both* made a mistake—then, like the civilized individuals they were, they could put it behind them. And go on.

He opened the door.

Josie looked up over the vases, a smile on her face. It faded at the sight of him. All the color in her face faded, too.

Sam's jaw clenched. He drew a careful breath. "Josie," he said, with what he hoped was the right blend of distance and camaraderie.

She swallowed. "Sam."

He felt as if he'd been slapped.

He was used to seeing Josie's face light up when he came in the room. He was used to a sparkle in her eyes, a grin on her face. There was no grin now, no sparkle. The look she gave him was shuttered. As remote as if she were standing behind a steel wall. He wasn't even entitled to the cheerful innkeeper persona that so endeared her to The Shields House clientele.

Well, fine. Sam pressed his lips together, then gave a curt jerk of his head, acknowledging the distance she'd put between them.

If that was the way she wanted it, so be it.

"I came as soon as I could," he said briskly. "I'm sorry I couldn't get to the funeral. I was in Hong Kong and I had to go to Japan before I came home."

"Of course." Josie picked up a carnation and with great care added it to one of the bouquets. She didn't look at him. She didn't say anything else. Not, How are you? Not, I've missed you.

The clock ticked. An airplane thrummed overhead. Sam drummed his fingers against his thigh.

"I should have been here for her. I should have come at Christmas. I didn't because…because…" *Of you.*

No, he couldn't say that. He sucked in a breath and tried again. "The last time I was here… I'm sorry about…"

He stopped there, too.

He owed her an apology, certainly. But she hadn't exactly been unwilling! He remembered that much. He wished to hell she'd look at him now, give him some indication of what she was thinking.

Sam Fletcher, who had once been told he "oozed charm through every pore," felt that at the moment he was oozing only sweat.

"About that night," he said finally, deciding that bluntness was the best policy. "It was a mistake. A *big* mistake…asking you to have a drink with me. And after…well, after…" He paused. *Damn it, at least look at me.*

She did. It was no help. Her face was so expressionless he didn't have a clue what she thought. Still, whatever he'd said so far, clearly it wasn't enough.

"I didn't mean… I never meant for what happened to…to happen." He stopped, flushing in the face of her total silence. "It was the whiskey talking…"

"I assumed as much." Josie's voice was flat, toneless. She turned to stare out the window.

"I tried to see you the next morning. I got a call from Elinor. I went to see you then, to tell you, before I left...but Hattie said you'd gone out with Kurt..." He looked at her for confirmation.

Her profile nodded.

So he hadn't screwed up her life. Thank God for that. He grinned shakily and breathed an enormous sigh of relief. "I'm glad."

"Are you?" She picked up the two vases in front of her and moved to put them on a cart. Sam watched, hoping she was wearing shorts so he could see those long, wonderful long legs—legs that had once wrapped around him and—

He didn't even notice her legs.

Only her belly.

Josie was pregnant!

And not just a little pregnant, either. She was *huge*.

"You're having a baby!"

Josie set the vases on the cart.

She was having a baby and— "And Kurt still hasn't married you?"

Suddenly Sam was furious. It was bad enough the jerk stood her up all the time! It was worse that he expected her to drop everything to type his damn papers! But this was ridiculous! "Just exactly how irresponsible is he?"

Josie turned to face him. "Why should he marry me? It's not *his* child."

"Not—?" Sam gaped, stunned. Not Kurt's child?

He scowled furiously, his mind ticking over, processing this new bit of information, trying desperately to sort things out, to put it together with what he knew about Josie Nolan.

He hadn't thought she was the type to sleep around!

She'd always seemed so quiet, so dedicated. Sweet. He'd always liked Josie Nolan, respected her, had always thought she'd got the short end of the stick in life and even in her choice of fiancés.

He'd felt sorry for her that night last autumn, had wanted to comfort her. Maybe he'd been wrong. His jaw locked. Just how the hell promiscuous was she?

"I trust you know who the father is?" he said acidly.

Josie's eyes widened. She went rigid. Her chin tipped up and Sam saw color flush her no longer expressionless face.

"As a matter of fact, I do," she said flatly. "You."

CHAPTER TWO

OH, WAY to go, Josie congratulated herself. Such tact. Such subtlety.

But it was hard to be subtle when you were as big as a rhinoceros.

Carefully, deliberately, she suppressed a sigh and strove to look as indifferent as she could. It wasn't easy. It was, in fact, even harder than she'd imagined.

For the last six months—ever since she'd realized that the night she'd spent with Sam Fletcher last September was going to have lasting repercussions of a more than emotional kind—she'd known this moment was coming. She'd put it off, resisting Hattie's continual exhortations to tell him, instead preferring to "stick her head in the sand," as Hattie called it.

Josie called it self-preservation.

What else would you call facing a man with the news that he was going to be a father when he was obviously unhappy about facing her at all?

Their night of intimacy had been "the whiskey talking." Hadn't he just said so? Of course he had. She'd known it at the time. She'd just been powerless to resist.

Josie Nolan had loved Sam Fletcher unrequitedly and hopelessly since she was fifteen years old.

A realist, Josie had never expected a drop-dead gorgeous millionaire jet-setter to fall madly in love with the foster-daughter of his aunt's next door neighbor. She might now be Hattie's protégée and innkeeper, but she'd started out as her cleaning girl. Josie had read Cinderella, but that didn't mean she was a fool.

But something must have.

Because when Sam Fletcher had appeared at her door the night of her twenty-fifth birthday, all misery, commiseration and gentleness, she'd been powerless to shut it in his face.

And so she'd spent the last six months trying to figure out how to tell him about the results of that night.

There had seemed no good way. Only ways that would have him think of her as a scheming hussy out to trap him into a marriage he didn't want.

At times—in the dead of night, for example, when she was remembering the tenderness of his touch, the urgency of his need, the firm persuasiveness of his lips— she tried to delude herself that there really had been something between them, that he'd welcome the news, that when he'd gone back to New York he'd missed her as much as she missed him.

In the clear light of day she knew that was so much hogwash.

But as long as he didn't show up and say it had been a mistake, she'd dared to hold on to a tiny ray of hope.

Not any longer.

"I never meant for what happened to…to happen," he'd said.

Neither had she.

But it had. And now they were going to have a child.

She stood now, waiting for him to ring a peal over her. To yell at her as Kurt had done. To turn bright red and point his finger at her, as Kurt had done. To say, "Well, what are you going to do about it?" in a hard, cold voice as Kurt had done.

"Mine?" Sam echoed. He wasn't red. He was dead

white under his jet-setter tan. And his voice wasn't cold.
It was hollow.

Still, he wasn't yelling. His tone was quiet. The quietness was momentarily reassuring. But looking at him
wasn't. He just stood there, looking as if a bomb had
gone off at his feet.

Josie supposed, to his way of thinking, it had. He'd
come prepared to deal with the inn and the animals, not
this.

"Yes," she said.

"You're sure?"

Her spine stiffened again, and the pang of concern
she'd felt for him vanished in a flash. Color burned in
her cheeks. "Yes, I'm sure. Despite the impression I
may have given, I do not ordinarily sleep around!"

"I didn't mean—" he began quickly, then stopped,
looked dismayed, then sighed and rubbed a hand over
his short sun-bleached hair. "Oh, hell, maybe I did. But
just because it was a shock. Sorry." This last was muttered.

He didn't look her in the eye. He couldn't seem to
stop slanting glances in the direction of her belly.

Josie took the apology in the spirit in which it had
been muttered—grudgingly. She picked up two more
vases and turned toward the cart. She wasn't just going
to stand there and let him gawk! And she didn't want to
watch the wheels turn in his head.

She would have liked to turn tail and run, but she was
damned if she was going to do that, either.

So she stayed, aware of the silence, aware of the foot-
shifting, aware of the eventual clearing of his throat.

"So…were you ever going to tell me?" His tone was
conversational now, almost casual, but she could hear
the strain in it and knew what control he was exerting.

She ran her tongue over her lips and shrugged in her own attempt at casual control. "Eventually I imagine I'd have had to."

"You'd have *had* to?" So much for casual. "You don't think maybe I'd have wanted to know?"

"To be honest, no."

He stared at her, jaw slack. Then, as if he realized it, he snapped it shut. His eyes never left hers.

Defiantly Josie stared back. "Well, under the circumstances, this isn't exactly a Hallmark moment, is it?"

A muscle in Sam's jaw worked. "Are you saying you don't want it?"

Josie pressed her hands protectively against her abdomen. "No, I am damned well not saying that! I want this child."

That was the one thing she was sure of. The daughter of indifferent, incompetent parents, she'd been abandoned, then passed from foster home to foster home since she was six. She wasn't having any such thing happen to her child. She was keeping it and taking care of it and loving it—and that was that.

"But I hardly imagine you do," she said frankly. "Do you?" she asked him, with the same bluntness he'd inflicted on her earlier.

He didn't answer for a moment.

She gave a satisfied nod, then turned on her heel and, pushing the cart toward the dining room, walked out the door.

Very little rattled Sam Fletcher.

Was he not a world-traveling entrepreneur of the highest caliber? Had he not negotiated with the pasha of a tiny west Asian kingdom with armed guards all around for the exclusive rights to a line of furnishings that his

competitors would give their eye teeth for? Did he not
routinely cope with multi-million dollar decisions upon
which the fate of many peoples' livelihoods—not the
least his own—depended? Had he not kept a calm de-
meanor when his fiancée was throwing him over for another man?

Yes, yes, yes, and yes again.

But being told you were the father of a woman's child
when you could barely remember bedding her—well,
that might ruffle the calmest of men.

Sam was beyond ruffled. He was moulting.

He stifled his first inclination, which was to tell Josie
Nolan that she had rocks in her head, that there was no
way he would be so irresponsible as to father a child on
a woman he wasn't married to! He knew his lack of
memory of what precisely had happened that evening
proved just how irresponsible he had been.

His second inclination was to run. To turn tail, head
out the door and never come back.

But Sam Fletcher did not run. He'd never run in his
life.

From the time he was a boy he'd been groomed to
face his responsibilities, to take charge, to exert leader-
ship, to do what was right.

He'd come to Dubuque today expecting to do what
was right. He'd expected to have to cope with the mare's
nest that usually comprised Hattie's affairs. He'd expected to have to find a buyer for the inn and even—
because Hattie wished it—to find homes for three cats,
a dog and a bird.

He'd envisioned showing up and, once the awkwardness of his apology was out of the way, laughing with
Josie about Hattie's having left him a woman.

It didn't seem funny at all now.

He hadn't expected a child.

The will had clearly been Hattie's way of doing what Josie had not done—of bringing him back and making him aware of the facts.

He supposed he ought to thank her for that. He would, if he weren't so rattled.

He was going to be a father?

That was rattling enough. What was worse was the idea that, without Hattie's will, he might never have known.

It was like waiting for the other shoe to drop.

All the while Josie was putting flowers in the rooms, checking in the guests, delivering champagne to the newlyweds, making dinner reservations and answering questions about local attractions, she was looking over her shoulder, expecting Sam to appear.

He hadn't been in the kitchen when she got back.

"Left," Cletus had said.

"Poleaxed 'im, did you?" Benjamin had said.

Josie had denied it, but she'd seen the look on his face. She wondered if they had seen the last of him. But, no. His rental car still sat by the curb. So, wherever he'd gone, he'd walked. She remembered he'd used to walk down to the yacht basin or along the river whenever he'd come here to think before.

"He needs space," Hattie had explained to her. "Perspective. He has to step back to understand his responsibilities."

Was that what he was doing now?

Whatever he was doing, Josie wished it didn't involve her.

She didn't know whether she wanted him to come back so they could get it over with—or whether she wished he'd stay away so she could pretend he never would.

Probably the former, she decided, unless he agreed to do the latter for the rest of her life!

But the rest of the afternoon passed—the guests checked in, the flowers got delivered, the guests got settled, the questions got answered and the reservations made—and there was still no Sam.

Good, she thought. No. Not good.

Damn. She didn't know what she wanted—except to tear her hair. She paced the front parlor. She peered out the windows. She even went out on the front porch and craned her neck to look down the road to see if she could see him, determined not to let him surprise her again.

But afternoon turned to evening and evening turned to dusk and eventually the cool of the mid-April evening made her retreat indoors. She paced some more in the parlor, then retreated to the kitchen, but the kitchen reminded her too much of their encounter this afternoon.

She headed down the steps to the basement laundry room. There were loads of towels and sheets to be folded. And if he came looking for her there, the stairs would creak and at least she'd hear him coming.

It was stupid to fret so much. Nothing was going to change even now that he knew. She would still be pregnant. Her love would still be unrequited.

She asked herself for the thousandth time why she couldn't have been satisfied with Kurt? Certainly he was a little too righteous and unbending for her taste. Certainly he thought his mission was more important than a wife.

But was he wrong?

He hadn't had to point out how foolish she'd been to taste forbidden fruit.

She made her way down the basement steps carefully, hanging on to the handrail. She'd used to trip down them thoughtlessly, light and easy on her feet. But with her new bulk and unaccustomed center of gravity, she had to move more cautiously.

Pity she hadn't moved more cautiously seven months ago.

She bent and fished a load of towels out of the bin, dumped them on the countertop and began to fold them. She made neat stacks and ran her hands over the soft terrycloth. It was mindless, mechanical work, soothing. She finished one stack, then bent to get another.

The baby kicked.

Josie smiled. Even when she was fretting most, this child could always make her smile. Perhaps it was silly to feel as if she had a confederate within, but she did. It was no longer Josie apart from the rest of the world. Now it was the two of them.

"Awake, are you?" she asked it softly. She set the towels down, rubbed a hand on her belly and was rewarded with another soft tap. She tapped back and smiled again. Sometimes she felt as if she was communicating in Morse code with this person who inhabited her body.

"Had a rough day?" she asked it. "I have. And it's going to get worse," she confided. She shook out a towel and gave it a snap before folding it.

The baby kicked again. Hard. So hard Josie winced.

"What's wrong?"

She nearly jumped a foot. She knocked the pile of freshly folded towels onto the floor and spun around to stare with equal parts horror and consternation in the direction of the wine cellar at the far end of the basement. Sam stood in the shadows.

"Now look what you've done!"

"That appears to be the least of what I've done," he said dryly as he stepped forward.

Instinctively Josie stepped back.

"What's wrong?" he repeated. "Are you hurt?"

She shook her head numbly. "No. It…it kicked, that's all."

"Kicked?" He looked blank.

"The baby."

He looked at her belly. She couldn't read his expression. He opened his mouth, as if he was going to say something. But then he just ran his tongue over his lips and shook his head. He bent to pick up the towels.

Josie watched him, dry-mouthed and silent, and wished she could push him aside and do it herself. She couldn't. There was too much baby between her and the ground. "What were you doing skulking in the wine cellar?" she demanded, indignant.

"I wasn't getting another bottle, if that's what you're worried about." Sam straightened and set the towels on the counter.

"You might as well put them in the wash again," Josie said crossly. "I can't use them now."

Obediently he dumped them in the washing machine. Then he answered her question. "I was thinking."

"In the wine cellar?"

"It seemed appropriate."

Josie pressed her lips together. She turned away and closed the lid of the washing machine, then reached past him to add soap, taking her time to measure it precisely. She set the dial to the right program. She had nothing to say.

Sam didn't move away. She continued to fuss with

the dial, then opened the lid again and checked the balance of the towels in the machine.

"I came because Hattie left me the inn," he said at last.

"I know." She didn't look at him.

"I'd thought she was going to leave it to you."

Josie shut the lid and gave the start button a push. "Why should she? I'm not family."

"You were closer to her than anyone. You were the granddaughter she and Walter never had. She loved you." He made it almost sound like an accusation.

"I loved her, too," Josie said fiercely, and turned her head to meet his gaze. "She was the mother—the grandmother—the family I never had. But I didn't ever expect her to leave me the inn! She did enough for me. She set up a trust fund. Mr. Zupper can tell you about it if you want. One for me and...and one for the baby."

"You were supposed to have the inn, too," Sam insisted. "When I was out here last fall—when Izzy... when I..."

"I know when," Josie said sharply. Did he think she'd forgotten?

Sam sucked in a sharp breath. "Okay, you know when. Well, back then she told me I wouldn't have to worry about the inn when she was gone. And I told her she wasn't going anywhere." He paused and Josie heard the ache in his voice. It matched her own ache, but she wasn't going to comfort him.

"You didn't know she was going to die," she said. "None of us did."

"Hattie did. She said, 'This old heart of mine could go any day. So I want you to know this.' And then she told me she meant no disrespect to the family, but she was going to leave it to you." He rubbed a hand against the back of his neck. "So when she left it—and you—to me, she was making a point."

Josie's head snapped around. "She left *me* to you?"

"I thought it was a joke."

A hell of a joke, Josie thought. But, "It is," she said firmly.

Sam shook his head. "No. She was right." He shifted from one foot to the other. His hands were jammed into his pockets. He looked at the floor for a long moment. The dryer swirled, the tap dripped. He lifted his gaze and met Josie's. "We'll get married."

As a proposal it left a lot to be desired.

In fact Josie felt as if he'd stabbed her in the heart.

We'll get married. Just like that. As if it were a foregone conclusion, a business negotiation with only one possible outcome.

She supposed where Sam Fletcher was concerned most business deals had only one possible outcome—the one he wanted.

But he didn't want this!

She knew he didn't want it. She could see it in his face, in his eyes. She heard it in the resignation in his voice.

And why would he? He didn't love her. He didn't want their child.

He was doing it because Hattie had forced his hand. He was doing it because he was used to doing the right thing, the necessary thing.

Just as Hattie had known he would.

Just as Josie had feared he would. It was why she wouldn't tell him about the baby.

"A child has a right to know its father," Hattie had said in a tone far more gentle than the bracing one she usually used.

"I know that," Josie had replied. "I just...can't tell him. Not now."

"When?"

"Sometime," Josie said vaguely.

"A father has a right to know his child, too," Hattie had gone on implacably.

"I'll tell him," Josie had promised. But she hadn't said when. And she'd changed the subject whenever Hattie brought it up.

"You can tell him at Christmas," Hattie had said eventually.

But Sam hadn't come. Josie had seen Hattie's disappointment when he hadn't come. She'd seen the older woman watching her with worry and concern in her eyes. But Josie had steeled herself against that concern because she knew *why* Sam hadn't come.

After that Hattie hadn't brought it up again.

Josie had dared to think Hattie had given up.

Obviously, once the will had been read, she knew she'd thought wrong. Hattie had made sure Sam would know.

Now Sam did know—and had done the very thing Hattie had hoped—and Josie had dreaded—he might.

It wasn't the way he'd imagined proposing marriage, standing in a laundry room, willing his prospective, very pregnant bride to look at him, his hands in his pockets, fists clenched.

It certainly wasn't the way he'd proposed to Izzy. That had happened at a cozy dinner at a candlelit table in a restaurant on the top of Knob Hill. They had been laughing together, touching, and his suggestion that what they had was too good to waste on casual moments had been enough to make Izzy catch her breath, then turn a thousand-watt smile in his direction.

This time he was standing stiffly, touching no one, his head bent beneath the stone basement's low ceiling. His voice was stiff and awkward. And, far from bestowing any thousand-watt smile, Josie was looking at him as if he'd just electrocuted her.

Surely it wasn't a surprise. She had to know what they had to do. It was the only responsible thing to do—though heaven knew if he could have thought of something else, he probably would have done it.

Besides, what did she expect? A profession of undying love? Hardly. Especially not after he'd already assured her just hours before that his actions that night had been a mistake.

It was enough that he was willing to do the right thing, he assured himself. He looked at her expectantly and waited for her to do the right thing, too.

She said, "No."

Sam gaped. He wasn't jet lagged this time, but he thought his hearing was going just the same. He checked. "No?"

"No. Thank you," she added after a moment, but he didn't think she sounded very grateful.

His jaw tightened. "Why the hell not?"

It wasn't as if he'd wanted to marry her, for heaven's sake! He was being a good sport, though, and making the offer. The least she could do, damn it all, was accept it!

"When I marry, I'm marrying for love," she said simply.

He stared at her. He glanced around the tiny laundry room pointedly, then at her now bare ring finger. "Forgive me if I'm wrong," he drawled, "but I don't see your own true love clamoring for a wedding date any longer.''

Josie got a tight, pinched look on her face and he immediately felt like a heel. "No," she admitted quietly, then blinked and looked down at her hands.

Oh, hell. It was like kicking a puppy.

"I didn't mean…" he muttered at last, his voice gruff. He started to reach for her, to comfort her, then remembered where that had got him last time. He pulled back sharply. "Sorry."

In fact, he wasn't sorry at all. This might not be the reason her engagement *ought* to have been broken, but Kurt Masters didn't deserve a woman as kind and generous and open and—well, hell—as *loving* as Josie. But he didn't suppose she wanted to hear that right now.

"Kurt doesn't matter," she said after a moment.

Sam wouldn't argue about that. "Glad to hear it," he said brusquely. "Then why are you saying no?"

"I told you."

"Because you want love." He fairly spat the word. "And what about the baby? Don't you want it to have love?"

Her nostrils flared. "Of course I do! What are you talking about?"

"You're depriving it of a father's love."

"You don't love it," she said flatly.

"How the hell do you know?"

"You can't."

"Why not?" He was incensed now, breathing down her neck.

"Because in the ten years I've known you I've never heard you express any desire for children whatsoever!"

"So maybe I changed my mind."

Josie rolled her eyes. "Give me a break."

"No, you give me a break. You're the one who's had all the time to get used to this. I've just had it sprung on me—"

"There was nothing stopping you coming back any time in the last seven months," Josie pointed out with saccharine politeness.

"I thought I was making both of us happy staying away!"

"You were."

He heaved a harsh breath. "And now I'm not. But I am being responsible. I am ready to do the right thing and—"

"And you're so sure you know what the right thing is?"

He opened his mouth. He hesitated.

The hesitation was all it took. Josie folded her arms across her breasts. "You don't want to marry me, Sam. You don't want a child. You want to sell the inn and get the hell out of here and you never want to look back. Isn't that right? Isn't that what you came for?"

"I came because Hattie left me holding the bag!"

"Exactly. And I'm telling you, you don't have to hold it any longer. Hattie wanted you here. Not me. It was a mistake, like you said earlier today." She started toward the stairs, then turned back and faced him squarely. "It was, as you said earlier, 'the whiskey talking.'"

"I didn't mean—"

"Yes, you did. You were honest. And now you're lucky. I'm not holding you accountable for what you did under the influence of whiskey."

"What if I want to be held accountable?"

Their eyes dueled once more.

Then, "Go to hell, Sam," Josie said, and stalked up the stairs.

Footsteps came after her. "Don't you walk out on me!"

Josie turned halfway up, color vivid on her cheeks. "Don't you yell at me," she said, in a voice quieter than his, but no less forceful. "Not if you want The Shields House to keep a good reputation."

"The hell with The Shields House!"

Josie shrugged. "Well, suit yourself. It's your house. Your business."

"I offered to share it with you."

"And I said no. Thank you," she added, the polite afterthought as damnably annoying as her refusal. "Don't slam the door when you leave." She turned then, and left him standing there.

Sam glared at her back until she went around the corner. Then he stomped into the kitchen, flung open the door to the entry hall and stalked out. He managed—barely—not to snarl at the guests in the parlor. But that was as far as his good behavior went.

There was no way, he thought as he banged out furiously, that you could have a satisfying argument if you couldn't even slam a door!

It had been every bit as bad as she'd feared it would be.

Worse.

He'd asked her to marry him. Because he was a gentleman. A responsible man. A kind man.

All the things she wanted in a husband—and couldn't have.

Because he didn't love her.

And he was honest enough not to lie and say he did. That was what made it worse.

Josie stood behind the curtain and stared out across the lawn. She could see Sam now, standing on the edge of the bluff that overlooked the city, his shoulders hunched, his hands jammed in the pockets of his jeans. The wind ruffled his short hair. He looked miserable.

He ought to be rejoicing.

She'd told him no, hadn't she?

Maybe it hadn't sunk in yet. When it did, he'd be glad.

Even then, though, he'd still feel responsible. He'd want to make things right. It was the way Sam was. The way he'd always been. Hadn't he come to console her the night Kurt had stood her up?

She shoved the thought away. She had done nothing but think about it for seven months. She'd hoped…she'd dreamed…she'd wished…she'd been the fool she'd promised herself she would never be. She had not been able to squelch the hope that he might have fallen in love with her.

He hadn't. And now it was over.

Tomorrow would be better for both of them. He would still try to do the right thing, of course, but it would be a reasonable right thing this time. He would offer child support, acknowledgement, a trust fund, perhaps. Her child would be weighted down with trust funds, she thought with a rueful smile.

Being Sam, he might ask for two weeks in the summer when he could see their child.

She wouldn't argue. It was his right. She would be polite and properly grateful. And he would be concerned and secretly relieved at having escaped the need to follow through on his proposal, but far too polite to let it show. It would all be very civilized.

And she would be tied to Sam Fletcher for the rest of her life.

It would be hard, but she would do it—for her child.

"Not for yourself?" she mocked herself now as she rocked back on her heels and looked down at the only man she had ever really loved.

If she was going to be scrupulously honest—she would admit that she didn't dislike the idea of having Sam still a part of her life.

It wasn't the same as marrying him. She didn't want any part of forcing him into a relationship which ought to be based on love.

But to know how he was, where he was, what he was doing...

Just to know...

She'd said no?

No?

Sam still couldn't believe it.

Or maybe he could. Women seemed to be developing a history of not wanting to marry him. First Izzy, now Josie. Was it getting to be a trend?

His jaw was clenched so tight he had a headache. He forced himself to take a deep breath. But he didn't relax. He paced along the bluff overlooking the downtown and didn't see any of it. He saw only the disaster the evening, the day—no, his whole damn life—had become.

He didn't think he was that hard to get along with. He certainly could keep any wife in the manner to which she'd never yet become accustomed. He wasn't all that bad-looking.

Was he?

No, damn it, he wasn't.

So what was the problem?

"'I want to marry for love,'" he muttered in a falsetto mockery of Josie's tone as he kicked a rock against the limestone wall that edged the bluff. "Well, hell, sweetheart, so do I. So *did* I."

But there was a child to think about now. *His* child. *Her* child.

Their child.

That child might owe its existence to circumstances that had been fogged by a little too much whiskey. But their lovemaking hadn't been a mindless, soulless coupling. He might not remember all that had happened that night, but his body had known, his emotions had known. He had responded to Josie and she had responded to him.

He was willing to bet she would still respond to him!

He looked over his shoulder at the house. On the upstairs landing, a curtain twitched. His jaw set, his eyes narrowed.

"You think the answer is no, Josie Nolan?" he told the woman he was sure was standing behind that curtain.

Well, Sam Fletcher never backed down from a challenge.

CHAPTER THREE

IT WAS fate, Josie decided.

Surely God couldn't have that warped a sense of humor. Surely in a twenty-odd room inn, He wouldn't deliberately stick Sam in the room next to hers tonight, in the bed right on the other side of the wall from hers—again—just for old time's sake!

She'd actually entertained the notion that she might get away with not having him stay at all.

The inn was fully booked—even the third-floor garret that had been hers while Hattie was alive. Just three days ago Josie had finished fixing it up as a guest room and, with Benjamin and Cletus's help, had moved her things down one flight into Hattie's quarters.

"You ought to be pleased," she'd told Sam when he realized the inn was full. "Another room to rent means more profit for you."

"The hell with profits. Where'm I going to sleep?"

He'd tapped on her door about ten and she'd opened it warily, but he hadn't said another word about marrying her. He'd been almost icily polite as he'd asked where he ought to put his things. The iciness had dissolved into irritation at the news that there were no rooms.

"I'll see if I can get you a room at The Taylor House." It was another Victorian era B&B. Not, in Josie's estimation, as nice as The Shields House, but still quite comfortable.

"I'll sleep in the sitting room," Sam said, looking past her toward the small room that was part of her quarters. Josie knew Hattie had sometimes put Sam there when all the other rooms were full.

But that had been Hattie. Not her. "I'm afraid not."

One brow lifted. "Why not? Did you rent that, too?"

Josie sucked in a breath. "I am trying to do my best to run your inn professionally, and that means renting the rooms. So I have. That doesn't mean I have to give up my own."

"You sleep in the sitting room?"

"It's part of my quarters," she said firmly. The inn-keeper's quarters consisted of two rooms—a bedroom and a parlor—and a bath. And, no, she didn't sleep in her sitting room, but she didn't want him sleeping there, either. It would be too intimate, too close.

"You certainly didn't waste any time moving in, did you? Hattie's been in her grave—what?—two weeks?"

His words hit her like a slap, and her reaction must have showed on her face, for he rubbed a hand against the back of his head and muttered, "Sorry. I didn't mean that. I'm not usually so tactless."

"No," Josie agreed, "you're not."

His gaze nailed her. "But then I don't usually dis-cover I'm about to become a father, either."

She pressed her lips together and hugged her arms across her breasts protectively, but she was damned if she was going to apologize. "I'll call The Taylor House."

"Don't bother. I'll sleep in the butler's pantry."

Josie's eyes widened. "You can't!"

"Why not? Did you rent that, too?"

"Don't be an ass, Sam. There's only a love seat down there."

"Badly named, I'm sure."

Josie ignored that. "You can't," she repeated.

"Well, if you won't let me use the sitting room..."
He was baiting her, daring her.

Josie gritted her teeth. "No."

"It's not like we haven't been closer than a room
apart..." A corner of his mouth lifted mockingly.

She felt her cheeks begin to burn. "I said, no!"

Sam took a step back and raised his hands, palms out,
as if to defend himself. "Fine. The butler's pantry for
me." He started toward the stairs.

"I'm calling The Taylor House!"

"Go ahead. I'm not leaving."

Josie watched him go, frustrated, annoyed, and determined not to give in. "Go ahead yourself! Sleep on the
love seat!" *Get a crick in your neck. Serve you right for
being so obstinate.*

She shut her door, barely managing to take her own
advice and not slam it. Then she retreated to her bedroom, determined to ignore him. She had one more couple left to arrive, who would be getting there late. Ordinarily she'd wait for them downstairs in the butler's
pantry, reading or watching television.

Obviously that wasn't an option tonight.

So she stayed in her room, alternately reading and
hauling herself up to pace irritably. When the phone rang
an hour later she snatched it up. The people who had
been scheduled for Coleman's Room couldn't make it.

"Sorry to call so late," they apologized. "Family
emergency."

"No problem," Josie assured them. Then she hung up
and closed her eyes. "Oh, damn."

She didn't have to do it. She almost didn't do it.

But Josie had spent enough nights in her life sleeping
in uncomfortable circumstances to have a modicum of

sympathy—even for Sam. Reluctantly, she went down to the butler's pantry.

It was dark, but in the moonlight spilling through the tall, narrow window, she could see Sam lying on the love seat, his legs dangling over the end.

"Come to see if I was comfy?" he drawled.

"Came to tell you that you can have Coleman's Room," she replied through her teeth. "The guests just canceled."

In the moonlight she saw the slow spread of his grin. Her very own version of the Cheshire Cat. Then he stretched expansively and hauled himself up. He was wearing only a pair of boxer shorts.

Josie had beat a hasty retreat up the steps.

Unfortunately, the image had stuck in her mind.

And having him in Coleman's Room was turning out to be worse than letting him sleep in her parlor would have been. Her parlor was on the other side of the bathroom. Coleman's Room shared a common wall with hers.

She crawled back into her own bed and tugged the duvet up to her chin. Resolutely she turned away from the wall. From the memory. From Sam.

It didn't help. She knew he was there.

Just like he'd been last time...

It was her birthday. September ninth. And she was determined that it would be the most special birthday she could remember.

For years she'd pretended an indifference to her birthdays. In foster families there were fewer disappointments if one didn't expect too much. Even when she'd lived with her own parents, things had been so unpredictable that Josie had learned not to expect.

When she'd come to stay with Hattie and Walter, they

had celebrated with her. That was as close to having a real family—and real birthdays—as she could remember.

Once, the year she'd turned fifteen, even Sam had been here for the celebration. He'd given her a gift.

Of course she'd known he hadn't picked it out especially for her. He'd been on his way back home from his first solo buying trip to the Orient and he'd stopped to see Hattie and Walter on his way.

It was the first time she'd met him. And the minute she did, her fantasies took on a whole new dimension. Next to the high school boys she knew, Sam was a god. Lean and lithe, not to mention more than a little handsome, he set Josie's heart to going double time. But it was more than his looks that attracted her. It was the enthusiasm with which he threw himself into helping Walter. She'd expected Sam would find scraping and painting Walter's boat beneath him. But he stripped off his shirt and pitched right in, laughing and talking to Walter—and sometimes even to her.

He and Walter compared what Walter called "sea stories"—tales of travels hither and yon. Josie had heard and enjoyed most of Walter's before. But she hung on every word of Sam's. He'd been everywhere, done everything—and enjoyed it all. Josie listened, enthralled. After that, she made sure that wherever he was, she wasn't far away.

He must have noticed—and enjoyed—her attention, for, on her birthday, after she'd opened the gifts Hattie and Walter had given her, Sam offered her a small square box.

"It's just something I picked up on my trip," he told her, almost apologetically, when she opened the box. "Not much."

To Josie it meant the world. She was stunned by the beauty of the tiny jade horse she found nestled inside. She caressed it with one careful finger, then smiled at it as it stood on the palm of her hand.

"Thank you," she told him, her heart in her eyes. "I'll treasure it."

He looked embarrassed. "No big deal."

But it was to Josie.

She still had that tiny horse sitting on her dresser. She still remembered that birthday as the best she'd ever had. She had dreamed of other birthdays with Sam to share them—for months afterward.

But eventually she grew up and realized that Cinderella stories didn't happen in real life.

And so she was pleased when Kurt began to come around. He wasn't gorgeous like Sam, but he was easy on the eyes. He wasn't well travelled like Sam, but he'd certainly been farther than she had. He was often preoccupied, rarely attentive. But he needed her, which was more than Sam did. That was a start.

She'd met Kurt when she'd baked cookies for a church bake sale. He'd snagged one off the plate, told her they were marvelous and asked if she'd bake him some as well. She'd baked a lot of cookies for him since, and gone to a lot of church suppers and typed a fair number of papers that Kurt didn't have time to type for his work on his Master of Divinity degree because he was, as he put it, "ministering to his flock."

Josie understood. She was flattered that he thought enough of her to want to spend his few free moments with her. It wasn't as if there were a lot of other men clamoring for her attention.

The only man she ever wished would was Sam Fletcher.

And then she learned he was engaged.

The despair she felt the afternoon that Hattie told her Sam was getting married astonished her. She hadn't *seriously* thought he'd ever be interested in her, had she?

Well, no, but...

But, until he'd got engaged, somewhere in the back of her mind she'd dared hope.

With Sam's engagement to Isobel Rule, Josie knew her dreams were dust. She hoped no longer. She focused on Kurt.

Still, she was stunned when he proposed to her in May.

"You want to get married? Us?" she said, not sure she'd heard right.

Kurt smiled and nodded, then leaned forward to brush a kiss across her lips. "Of course, us," he said. "Why not? We make a good team."

And, indeed, Josie thought, why not? They did make a good team: Kurt took care of the world, and Josie took care of Kurt.

"Do you love me?" she asked him.

"Of course I love you."

She knew what he meant. Kurt loved everyone.

When she was alone, later, she said their names together. "Kurt and Josie. Josie and Kurt." She liked the sound of it. It made her feel a part of something.

And if it didn't have the same ring as "Sam and Josie"—well, she really hadn't expected that, had she?

And she did love Kurt the way he loved her.

So she said yes. They planned to get married the following year, after Kurt got his Master's and found a church. It seemed a long time, but Josie didn't mind waiting. They were still a couple.

For Kurt's birthday in July she got them reservations

at a romantic riverside restaurant. She took a long time deciding on gifts for him, finally getting him the collected works of a theologian he particularly admired and a CD by the jazz group he liked that he'd gone to see in Chicago. She also knitted him a sweater in shades of blue that brought out the depths of his eyes and baked him a batch of his favorite butterscotch cookies.

He was delighted. He kissed her and told her how much it meant to him—how much *she* meant to him. And then he apologized because they wouldn't be able to use the dinner reservations. He had a church meeting to go to.

Josie understood. She smiled gamely and canceled the reservations. There would be other times, she assured him—and herself.

"Of course there will," he promised. "We'll go on your birthday."

She hugged the thought to herself and, when her September birthday rolled around, Josie made the reservations again.

Maybe she should have let Kurt do it. If she had, he might have remembered.

She reminded him. The night before, as he left after coming to eat supper and pick up the paper she'd typed for him, she said, "Don't forget dinner tomorrow night. Six-thirty."

"Dinner," he said absently, and dropped a kiss on her forehead.

She watched him walk down the drive, his head bent, his eyes already scanning down the work she'd done.

"What are you cooking him tomorrow night?"

The sound of Sam's voice behind her made her jump. She'd thought she'd got used to him being in the house. He'd come almost two weeks before, silent and morose, and had thrown himself into working at whatever Hattie asked him to do.

Josie had waited for him to explain, but he hadn't. He'd just sawed and banged and hammered.

The explanation had come from Hattie. "His engagement is off."

Josie had tried desperately to ignore the leap of joy in her heart. In fact she'd tried desperately to ignore *Sam*. She didn't want to love him anymore. He didn't know she was alive. It was foolish to care. Besides, she had Kurt.

She ignored the sarcasm in Sam's voice. "Nothing," she said airily. "He's taking me out."

"Does he know that? You picked the place and made the reservation."

"Because I want to go there," she said through her teeth, "and Kurt's very busy."

"With everyone but you."

"He has time for me," she maintained stoutly. "All tomorrow night."

Sam snorted. "If he remembers."

She knew he had witnessed Kurt's absent-mindedness more than once over the last two weeks, and he made a point of saying so. He never said anything about the good Kurt did for his parishioners.

Josie knew her fiancé wasn't perfect. But it wasn't as if Sam had picked such a great fiancée himself. After all, Isobel had dumped him!

"Don't worry about me," she said.

"I won't." Sam turned on his heel and walked out.

Kurt wouldn't forget, Josie told herself. Of course he wouldn't. He knew how much this celebration meant to her.

On the night of her birthday, she made dinner for

Hattie and Sam, but declined to eat with them. Instead she went upstairs to get ready to go. Then she sat in the parlor and waited, smiling cheerfully as she chatted with the guests. Six-thirty came and went. So did seven. Her smiles got to be a little more distracted. Her replies to the guests' comments were just a little vague.

Sam came through on his way up from the wine cellar and raised a bottle in toast to her still sitting there. Josie looked away.

At seven forty-five she excused herself and went out on the porch, still smiling, but a little worried. Kurt's car wasn't the newest or in the best shape. Could he have been in an accident?

She peered down the road. She walked to the edge of the bluff and looked to see if she could see his car. She waited outside until eight-thirty. Alone.

Finally, at nine, she gave up. She hurried through the parlor, head down, glad that Sam wasn't there to smirk at her.

Hattie looked up from peeling apples and frowned. "Back already."

Josie managed a smile. "I never left. He must have had an emergency come up." She wished her voice didn't waver.

"He didn't call," Hattie translated.

"He probably couldn't get to a phone. Here, let me do that," Josie said. She almost snatched the peeler out of Hattie's hand and set to work.

She needed to be busy, not to think. Not to hurt.

After the casseroles were assembled and in the refrigerator, she set the table. She folded the napkins into swans, then unfolded them again and made doves. She polished the coffeepot, the teapot, the tray, the creamer and sugar bowl. And all the while she listened for his footsteps and blinked back the stinging beneath her eye-lids.

Come, Kurt, she prayed silently. *Please, come.*

He never came.

She told herself he had a good reason. She was being silly to care so much. It was ridiculous to be so hurt.

But she was. The pain was there, knotted tight inside her. And so—once she gave up hoping and sought the solitude of her room shortly after eleven—were the tears.

Josie wasn't ordinarily a weeper. Ordinarily she was a stiff-upper-lip, nothing-gets-me-down kind of girl.

But tonight she wept.

She took off the gauzy rose-colored dress she'd bought specially for the evening. She ran her tongue over her lips as she hung it in the closet, then shut the door. She went into the bathroom and washed her face and brushed her teeth. She took her hair down out of the French braid she'd laboriously done it up in that after-noon and shook it out, loose and billowing around her head. And all the while she swallowed, blinked, kept the tears at bay.

But when she put out the light and slid under the covers, they came.

Slowly, one by one, tears slipped from beneath her lids. She tried to stop them. She choked on them, gulped them, swallowed desperately, commanded herself to quit. But there was no quitting this time.

She cried.

She cried for the missed dinner, the lonely birthday, the hopeful fool she'd been, the silly goose she was. She cried for the little girl who'd always been on the outside looking in. She cried for the young woman who didn't seem to matter to anyone.

She didn't know how long she cried. But finally, vaguely, she became aware of a soft tapping on her door.

She gulped frantically, trying to silence the sobs, to get a grip on herself. The last thing she needed was for one of the guests to hear her! They couldn't have, could they?

No, of course not. The room next to hers was the one where Sam was staying—and he wouldn't have been hanging around on a Saturday night. It was probably the people staying in the Ballroom, needing an extra pillow or a coffee carafe or one of the portable phones. She'd told them when she checked them in where her room was and that if they needed anything to call on her.

Josie swiped the tears from her cheeks, scrubbed at her face with the sheet, and, pulling on a robe and pasting her innkeeper smile on her face, she opened the door.

It was Sam.

She stared, nonplussed.

"You all right?" His voice was as soft as his knock had been, and there was none of the smirking smugness she'd expected. He looked a little ragged himself, his hair mussed as if he'd been running his fingers through it, his short-sleeved shirt unbuttoned and hanging open over a pair of faded jeans. He shifted from one bare foot to the other.

Josie stifled a sniff and nodded, blinking. "Of course I'm all right."

"I heard you crying."

She wanted to deny it. She didn't want Sam Fletcher knowing her weakness. The trouble was, he already did.

She gave an awkward little shrug. "It's no big deal."

"He stood you up?" There was no censure in his voice, not even the little bit that Hattie had used. He sounded sad.

Josie gave another shrug. "I'm sure he had a good reason."

He hesitated. Then, "I'm sure he did," Sam said quietly. Again she listened for the sarcasm she was used to from him where Kurt was concerned; again she failed to hear it.

"Did you want something?" she asked finally.

He lifted one hand and she noticed the bottle he was carrying. It wasn't wine. It was a bottle of Irish whiskey. "They say that misery loves company," he said. "Come have a drink with me."

Josie frowned. "A drink?"

"It's your birthday, isn't it? Let's celebrate." His voice was ragged, and Josie, who had a few more wits about her now, looked at him more closely.

"Are you drunk, Sam?"

"Not yet." He brandished the bottle again. "But I'm working on it."

"Why?"

"Come on, Josie. You gonna sit here and feel sorry for yourself all night? It's only your birthday, not your wedding night. You're not the only one who's ever been stood up, you know."

And then she understood.

In her own self-absorption, she'd completely forgotten that today was the day Isobel Rule was marrying another man.

She felt a surge of protectiveness toward the one standing in front of her. Handsome, strong, clever, tough, perfect Sam. Sam—the man she'd loved from a distance for years. How could Isobel have preferred anyone else to him?

"Oh, Sam." She shook her head helplessly.

He scowled, taking her words as a refusal. "It's not

good to drink alone. You don't want me to have to do it, do you?'' A corner of his mouth lifted ruefully. "It's Walter's best," he confided, nodding at the bottle. "I got it from the stash my esteemed great-grandfather toasted them with at their wedding. Only five bottles left."

Josie's eyes widened. Those bottles were practically sacred. "And you took one?"

"Hattie doesn't care. And it seemed appropriate." He hoisted the bottle once more. "I had to toast the bride's happiness, didn't I?"

"Oh, Sam," Josie said again. The wistfulness in his voice and the love she'd fought against all these years combined to swamp the last vestiges of her good sense.

Shutting the door to her room, she stepped out and padded the few feet down the hall to his.

In her mind—in her heart—in her dreams—she had been in his room before. She'd smiled at him, toasted him, touched him. This was reality, she reminded herself, and she didn't dare do any such thing!

Not mention the fact that she was an engaged woman.

Sam pushed open the door he'd left ajar, then stepped back so she could go in. For an instant Josie hesitated. But only for an instant. No more.

She didn't want to be alone tonight. No more than Sam did.

They'd both been dumped. They could console each other. Smile at each other. Sip a little of Walter's wonderful whiskey together.

What would it hurt?

Sam followed her in and shut the door.

The Captain's Quarters was one of the smaller rooms. But it seemed smaller now than it ever had, with the fire flickering in the fireplace and the whirlpool bath in the turret, and the canopied brass bed that suddenly looked bigger than it had when she made it up in the mornings.

Sam was pouring two glasses of whiskey. She could see that the bottle was almost empty. Good, she thought. She wouldn't lose her head.

"Sit down."

Josie looked around. The rocker was piled with books and papers and merchandising invoices. There was nowhere to sit—but the bed.

She ran her tongue over her lips, looked hopefully once more at the rocker as if it might suddenly dump its contents on the floor just for her. It didn't.

Sam was looking at her, waiting for her to sit. If she moved everything off the rocker he would think she was crazy. Obviously he didn't think about her in connection with beds!

She took a steadying breath and sat as if the bed might explode beneath her. But when it gave gently, and she felt like an idiot sitting primly on the edge, she pushed herself back up against the pillows, then held out her hand for the glass.

He gave it to her. Their fingers brushed for an instant, no more. But she felt electricity in his touch.

Oh, Josie, you fool. You dreamer.

Sam set the bottle on the bedside table and lifted his glass in the timeless gesture of a toast. A corner of his mouth tipped. "To them," he said.

Josie knew who he meant. Kurt for her. Isobel for him.

She tipped the glass against her lips. The fiery liquid touched her tongue, burning and numbing at the same time. Her eyes, fixed on his, watered. She swallowed.

So did Sam. Then he ran his tongue over his lips and, his eyes never leaving hers, he said, "To us."

Us?

Josie stared. Gulped. Trembled. But Sam was already taking another long swallow. So she did, too. *To us.* She could feel the last swallow flaming clear to her toes. This one seemed to soften, to soothe, to mellow. Her fingers tightened around the glass. Sam loomed over her.

"Shove over," he said.

Josie stared, then moved to do what he said. He sat down and swung his legs up, then leaned back, his shoulder pressing hard against hers. She could feel the warmth of his body through the thin cotton of her robe and his shirt. It felt hotter than the trail of the whiskey. She tried to edge away. Sam caught her knee in a firm grip.

"Don't," he said, his voice rough. "Stay."

Josie turned her head. His deep brown eyes were only inches from hers. His mouth was almost on a level with hers. Even in the firelight he was close enough that she could see each individual whisker that shadowed his jaw, could see the tiny chip in his front tooth that he'd once told her had come from a childhood fall, and the almost imperceptible chicken pox scar by his mouth that turned into a dimple when he smiled. Only Sam Fletcher could turn a chicken pox scar to advantage. She wanted to touch it.

It was too dangerous.

She took another quick desperate swig of Walter's whiskey. The danger receded.

It was only Sam. Nothing would happen between her and Sam. In ten years nothing ever had.

And then he kissed her.

She thought it was the whiskey, befuddling her brain, making her hallucinate. The touch of his lips against hers was soft and warm. Softer than the whiskey. Warmer.

Smoother. Gentler. It didn't scorch. But the heat was there. Slow and steady. Like kindling catching fire, flickering, growing, then settling into a full-blown blaze.

Sam was kissing her!

It was folly, she told herself. It was foolishness. It was wrong.

It was Sam.

Her lashes fluttered shut. Her lips parted. She tasted his lips, his tongue. Her own resisted, but not for long. Her lips nibbled, too. Just for a moment. Just to see. Just to touch. Just to taste.

He tasted good. Better than good. Wonderful. And when his lips left her to trail along her jaw and cheek, she whimpered, wanting him back. But the soft rasp of his rough cheek against her jaw felt almost as good as his mouth had. Her whimper turned into a purr.

The ache of need that had been building inside her so long she couldn't remember when it had begun, now seemed to flower, to open and respond to his touch.

This is Sam! she told herself. *Sam!*

Her mind did its best to shout a warning. But her body just said, *Yes. Yes, it is.* And her heart—heaven help her—seemed only to say, *At last.*

Her mouth, which had more sense than the rest of her, did manage to say, "We shouldn't—" and her arms even tried to push him away.

What was she supposed to say—or do—when he agreed? When he said, "I know. I know," but didn't stop? When he kept on with those soft, gentle kisses, and each one was better than the last?

It felt right to be in his arms.

When, she wondered, had she come to be in his arms? No matter. She was there. Snug. Secure. Safe.

Safe?

No, one glass of whiskey hadn't muddled her mind that badly.

"Sam, we can't—"

"Shh," he whispered against her lips. "We won't."

Then he did pull back. He shoved himself far enough away to fill their glasses again, then to draw her hard against him inside the curve of his arm. He rested his cheek against the top of her head. "We won't," he said again, his voice soft and ragged. He took a sip.

So did Josie.

"He's a fool," he said at last. He took her hand in his, folding them together, making them one.

"So's she," Josie whispered, giving his fingers a squeeze.

She felt him smile slightly against her hair. "She didn't think so."

She wanted him to look at her. She reached up a hand and touched his cheek, drew a line along his jaw. He turned back again. He was so close her lashes brushed his cheek. She couldn't see. She kissed instead.

It was odd, really, how one moment she could be thinking that their earlier kiss had been an aberration— a once in a lifetime experience—and the next she could feel as if kissing Sam was the one thing in life she'd always been waiting for.

"I'm sorry," she breathed against his mouth. "So sorry." For his hurt, she meant. For the pain that Isobel caused him.

Not for this.

She should be sorry for this. She was a fool not to be. She shouldn't ache for him, but for herself.

Perhaps she did.

Perhaps she was sorry for both of them, and that was why she kissed him. And let him kiss her. Again.

And again.

It was one of the fantasies she'd woven for herself over the years: the fantasy in which Sam finally noticed her, awakened to the woman she'd become—and wanted her.

The kisses changed. They had little to do with comfort now and less to do with compassion. She wondered when they had stopped saying, *I'm sorry Kurt didn't want you,* and started saying, *I want you myself.*

She didn't know, but she knew there was hunger in his mouth this time when it touched hers. There was an urgency and persuasion in the way it covered hers, seeking, dipping, tasting. It hoped. It asked. It demanded.

Josie understood the demand. She felt it herself. She didn't know when she forgot to remember Kurt. She didn't know when she forgot her birthday and her loneliness and her dreams. But it wasn't long before they all faded before the reality of the moment.

Of Sam.

When his hands began to roam over her body, smoothing and touching, learning her lines and her curves, she gave herself up to the sensation. She let him touch because she wanted to be touched. By him.

She never pretended it was Kurt touching her. The whiskey might have lowered her resistance, but it didn't muddy her thinking. She knew whose fingers skimmed over her nightgown. She knew whose body shifted and hardened, whose breath tickled her cheek and whose mouth touched hers. She knew.

And she knew that she didn't care.

Or perhaps she cared too much—about the wrong man. About Sam.

She didn't know what Sam knew. Or what he pretended. Or how much he cared.

For the moment just having him in her arms was enough. She reveled in the sensation of the slightly rough pads of his fingers as they trailed along her arm. She shivered as they slid over her breast and parted the front of her robe, loosing the sash and opening it further.

But then it wasn't enough. Josie needed to touch him, too.

She set the glass aside and tentatively ran her hand over his arm, loving the silky feel of the sun-bleached hair that roughened the skin there. She eased her hand across his arm to touch the soft cotton of his shirt, then slipped past it to caress the hard flesh of his chest.

She'd never touched Sam's chest before. Had wished to, had dreamed of it. But never until now had she dared.

It was warm. It was silky and firm. Hair-roughened, like his arms. Strong, like his arms. She'd told herself Sam was a corporate pencil-pusher but he had the body of a man who worked with his muscles for a living. What did he do when he wasn't pushing pencils or flying around the world on an airplane?

She didn't know. She wanted to.

She wanted to know everything about him. What he thought, what he hoped, what he dreamed, what every inch of his body felt like under her touch.

He slid her robe off. His head was bent over her breasts as he dropped light, moist kisses through the thin cloth, his hot breaths teasing her flesh beneath the damp cotton. She felt shivers of anticipation, of need. She clenched one hand against his hair, gripping the back of his neck and arching her body closer to his.

He fumbled with her nightgown, sliding it up above her hips. She knew if she was going to stop him that it had to be now. And even as she knew it she knew she was wrong—the moment to stop him was past. He couldn't stop now.

And neither could she.

Perhaps she'd been kidding herself, thinking she could marry Kurt. She loved him, of course she did. But like a brother, *never* like this.

The feelings Sam was provoking in her tonight had been building since time out of mind. They were so strong they seemed inevitable. Preordained.

He groped to unfasten the button on his jeans, but his fingers behaved like so many thumbs. He muttered a soft curse and shook his head. His fingers trembled.

Josie smiled. "Let me."

He stilled, his head dropped against her shoulder, his breath coming quick and harsh while she wrestled to undo the button of his fly and ease down the zipper. Her fingers brushed the urgent press of flesh beneath his briefs and she heard him suck in his breath sharply.

As soon as she had his jeans unfastened, he shrugged them off, then kicked off his briefs.

Now it was Josie's turn to draw in a sharp breath. She'd seen Sam in swimming trunks. She'd imagined often enough the masculinity concealed beneath them. But the reality of a wholly naked Sam Fletcher was worth appreciating.

Unfortunately there wasn't time. Not when the wholly naked Sam Fletcher was raising himself over her and settling in between her thighs. Not when she was wrapping her arms and her legs around him, learning—and loving—every warm hard inch of him.

She had never done this with Kurt, had never done it with any man. She should have been frightened, should have been wary. She should have fumbled, stumbled, panicked. She didn't.

Because no matter how wrong she might later think it was, at the time it only seemed right. Because it was Sam—and because even if her mind knew she was making a mistake, her heart knew she'd loved him since the beginning of time.

There was pain, quick and sharp. Sudden stillness as Sam braced himself above her, a look of shock, of sudden recognition in his eyes. They met hers.

Time stopped.

Sam stopped. A fine desperate tremor shook his body. He shuddered with the strain of holding so still. She saw him swallow, saw him bite down hard on his lower lip, holding himself back.

With one finger she lightly traced the hairline at the nape of his neck.

He quivered. He arched his back. His eyes shut tight in his taut face. She eased her hand around and touched his cheek. "Sam," she whispered, and drew a line toward his mouth. "My Sam."

His control snapped.

"Ah, Josie," he muttered, and dropped his head against her shoulder, then surged into her fully. And as Josie's pain faded her need grew, and she arched up to meet him, to complete him.

She felt him shatter in her arms and drew him close, held him and pressed her face into his shoulder even as he did the same to her. A series of gentle shocks seemed to ripple out from the core of her. There were no fireworks. There was no cataclysm.

But, heaven help her, there was love.

And, because she was a fool, there still was.

Because she was a fool, knowing that he was lying

only a few inches from her, albeit on the other side of a wall, Josie remembered—and relived that love again.

The more fool she, because clearly he hadn't loved her.

She'd learned that quickly enough.

Oh, for the remainder of that night she'd been able to fool herself into believing that he did. She'd stayed in his room, in his bed, holding him in her arms as he slept, and she'd told herself that everything would be all right.

In the morning she would tell Kurt that their engagement had been a mistake. She wasn't the girl for him. It was only the truth. She'd agreed to the engagement after she'd learned that Sam was going to marry Isobel. Why not? she'd thought, though perhaps not in so many words.

Perhaps she'd even convinced herself that what she felt for Kurt was love. Perhaps it was. But not the sort of love she felt for Sam.

She'd had no power against him that night. When he'd come to her, she could not have said no.

And now she was paying the price.

Marry Sam?

Once she'd thought it was the only thing that would ever make her really happy. Now she knew that to marry him when he loved another woman would be the quickest trip to heartbreak she could take.

No, she'd said. No.

She said it again now. "No." The sound was faint and empty in the stillness of the night. She tried to hang on to it.

He would be glad, she told herself. He didn't love her. It had been the whiskey talking that night—whiskey and misery and a loneliness he'd needed to assuage.

"No." She said it again, more strongly.

She should have said it seven months ago and she knew it.

She knew equally well that she was glad she hadn't. She pressed her hand to her taut, distended abdomen where Sam's child curled beneath her heart.

Only to their child did she dare to say yes.

CHAPTER FOUR

JOSIE was three breakfasts away from sanity when she tripped over Humphrey Bogart and dropped the apple cinnamon French toast all over the kitchen floor. "Damn!"

It was the last straw.

She'd been awake most of the night tossing and turning. She'd been remembering—*reliving*—and listening to Sam toss and turn, too. The walls were thin enough, the beds were close enough—or perhaps she was simply attuned enough—to hear him in the next room.

What had he been thinking?

She didn't want to know. Her own thoughts were disturbing enough. And the baby seemed to have sensed her distress for it had been equally restless. It seemed she had barely closed her eyes when the alarm pealed at six-thirty.

Slapping it into silence, Josie had staggered up and got dressed, being careful not to look at her ghastly reflection in the mirror while she combed her hair and brushed her teeth. Then she'd crept down the stairs to put breakfast on.

She had four guests doing a daylong bike ride on the Heritage Trail—the path along an old rail bed leading west from Dubuque to Dyersville. They'd asked for an early breakfast so they could leave by eight.

Josie generally had no trouble coping with such requests. This morning she could barely function.

She'd cut her thumb making fruit cups and bled into

the bananas. She'd thrown them out. Then she'd burned a pan of sausages. At the rate she was going, Sam would fire her and she could be the one who would leave.

She'd given Errol Flynn Wallace Beery's slimming food by mistake and spent half an hour tripping over the complaining cat before she'd realized it. Then she'd forgotten that one of her guests was a vegetarian, and had to dash out to retrieve the nicely browned sausages, apologizing because she'd been told and usually she didn't make mistakes like that. Dashing wasn't the simple proposition it used to be, either, now that she had a front seat passenger. She'd misgauged where the counter ended and bumped hard into it. To thank her for the bruise, the baby had kicked her.

Five more guests had appeared at the table before she had been ready for them. And then four more before she'd got those fed.

The last three were late, thank goodness, and she had been ready for them—until Humphrey Bogart got in the way and sent French toast and sausages and Josie all over the kitchen floor.

"Oh, drat!"

But before she could do more than gasp, strong arms were lifting her. Sam had her upright in an instant, but he didn't let go. It was the first time he'd touched her since the night they'd made love, and, while Josie had been telling herself she didn't want him, one touch and a night's worth of effort went right out the window.

"Are you all right?"

Shaken as much from his proximity as from her tumble, Josie jerked back. "Fine! I just fell over the dog." She tried to slip out of his grasp, but he hung on.

"You're sure?"

"Yes, of course." It hadn't been much of a tumble,

and she hadn't landed on her belly. Bumping her hip against the cabinet as she went down had broken her fall, though it would probably leave a bruise. Still, it wasn't rattling her nearly as much as he was.

"Please," she said, "let me go. I have to serve breakfast." *I have to get away from you.*

"You have to sit down."

"No, I—"

But Sam turned her, took her by her shoulders, and steered her not toward one of the kitchen chairs but right out the door and into the tiny butler's pantry. He aimed her at the love seat. "Sit."

"I can't! I have to—"

"You have to do what I tell you."

"Why should I?"

Sam gave her an equable smile. "Because I'll fire you if you don't."

She scowled. "Trust you to pull rank."

"Whatever it takes," he said mildly. "If it will make you feel better to fight about it, by all means, go ahead." He gave her a gentle shove and she toppled back onto the love seat. "But fight sitting down."

She started to struggle up, but the love seat was deep and the baby was pressing down on her. "The guests need their breakfast!"

"The guests will get their breakfast—as soon as I don't have to stand over you making sure you stay put." He tapped a foot so she could see how impatient he was to begin serving. Yeah, right.

Josie narrowed her eyes at him and did her best to look disapproving. Sam didn't budge. He just kept looming. She had the feeling he would stay there all day if she kept arguing with him.

"Someone has to clean up," she said.

"Not you."

She opened her mouth to argue, but his brows drew down in a fierce frown.

"Josie. Enough."

Exasperated, she said, "Fine. Do it yourself. Serve. Clean." She folded her arms across her breasts. "Stand on your hands and whistle Dixie, for all I care."

He grinned.

Sam Fletcher had a heart-stopping grin. Quickly she turned her head and reached to pick up a magazine, feigning indifference.

"That's better." Sam gave a nod of satisfaction. Then, still grinning, he turned and headed for the kitchen—whistling Dixie.

Josie sat on the love seat and fumed for the better part of an hour, listening to the murmur of Sam's voice as he talked to the guests. She wished she knew what he was saying, but she couldn't hear. Probably what a clumsy oaf she was, she thought irritably.

She started to stand and go to the door to listen, but her legs felt oddly rubbery. Had the fall rattled her more than she'd realized? The baby stirred inside her womb, stretching, then thumping.

"You are all right, aren't you?" Josie asked it worriedly. She sat very still, nervous now, waiting to see if she felt anything that might remotely be described as a contraction.

She'd had some lately. The first few times she'd felt a sort of vague tightening across her abdomen she hadn't known what it was. The last time she was at the doctor's she'd asked.

"Contractions," he'd told her. "A few irregular ones

won't hurt. You don't want them coming steadily, though. Not yet. Too early."

"It's still too early," she told her unborn child now. "Much too early."

They had two months to go yet. Josie kept her hand lightly against her abdomen, as if by doing so she could stop them coming. She felt the baby shift again, but that was all. Josie breathed a sign of relief.

Plates clattered in the sink. She heard silverware follow. Breakfast must have adjourned. A cupboard door banged. There was a hiss and an indignant meow. Sam cursed.

The door opened and Sam strode into the room, depositing a protesting Errol Flynn in Josie's arms. "Here. Take him. Keep him. I'll be right back with the other two. And the dog. I don't know how you haven't killed yourself in there. Those damn animals are underfoot every minute."

"I'm used to them." Josie put a protective arm around a still annoyed Errol.

"Well, I'm not." Sam started back into the kitchen, then stopped. "How are you doing?" The sudden gentleness in his voice cut right through to her heart.

She tried desperately to fend it off. "Fine. I told you."

"I'll bring you a cup of tea."

"I don't need—"

But apparently he didn't care what she didn't need. He left. Moments later he was back, with Wallace Beery and Clark Gable in his arms and Humphrey Bogart tagging along behind.

"They won't stay," Josie began.

"They will." He went out and came back with a treat for the dog and a bowl of milk for the cats.

"They aren't supposed to have milk."

"They aren't supposed to be underfoot, either. It's a trade-off."

Josie frowned at him. But the cats seemed pleased. Errol wiggled in her arms until she let him go. Then he hopped down and joined Wallace and Clark around the milk bowl. They all purred. Humphrey looked at Sam and wagged his tail, obviously hoping for another biscuit. Sam gave him one.

"Bribery," Josie groused.

He flashed her that damnable grin again. "Whatever it takes." Then, giving her a wink that she pretended not to notice, he shut the door between the kitchen and the sitting room and left her alone with the menagerie.

"'Whatever it takes,'" she said in irritable mockery.

The door opened again. He was back. "Milk, no sugar. Right?"

At her startled nod, he was gone again.

She slumped against the love seat, rocking back and forth. "Go away," she said softly. "Please, please. Just go."

She thought he'd forgotten. It was ten minutes at least. She was glad. Relieved. And then the door opened again and he was there, holding out a cup of tea.

"Thank you." She said the words warily. She *was* wary. But she was also thirsty. She took a sip. An involuntary shiver of pleasure coursed through her.

"All right?"

Josie nodded, not trusting her voice.

"That's okay, then." He gave her a crooked smile. His hand lifted slightly, opened, then closed into a fist. He turned to go back to the kitchen.

Josie watched him leave and felt tears pricking behind her eyelids. The lump in her throat grew even bigger.

"All right?" she asked herself, just as he had.

No, it wasn't all right. It wasn't all right at all.

"Every young woman should have a husband like yours," Mrs. Jensen said as she handed over her credit card later that morning.

Josie almost ran the slide of the credit card terminal right over her fingers. *"What?"*

"Such a thoughtful young man. He told us he was serving breakfast so you could rest."

"Um," Josie said. "Yes, well, he was a little... insistent."

"Enjoy it, dear," Mrs. Jensen urged her. "Not every man is like yours."

"No." Josie had no trouble acknowledging that. She fumbled with the charge slip and handed the credit card back.

Mrs. Jensen patted Josie's hand. "It's so thoughtful of him to have your rings resized, too."

Josie's ringless fingers jerked. "My rings?" she echoed wildly, her eyes bugging.

"Oh, dear. Perhaps I shouldn't have said. Do you suppose he meant it to be a surprise?"

Josie shook her head numbly. *Rings? What rings?*

"I noticed you weren't wearing your wedding ring," Mrs. Jensen confided. "So I asked him if you'd had the same trouble I had during my pregnancy. My hands and feet swelled up like sausages. I thought the same thing was happening to you."

Josie felt an uncomfortable warmth steal into her cheeks. She made a vain effort to pull her hand out of Mrs. Jensen's grasp, but the older lady hung on.

"And Sam—that is his name, isn't it?—Sam said, yes, you had gotten quite puffy so he'd taken the rings to be resized."

"P-puffy?" Josie sputtered.

Mrs. Jensen beamed. "That's kinder than Tom here—" She cast a fond glance over her shoulder at her husband. "He just told everyone I was getting fat."

"Here, now, I never..." Mr. Jensen protested.

But Mrs. Jensen laughed. "Don't worry, my dear. I slimmed down again right after the baby came. I'm sure you will, too," she said to Josie, and gave her hand one last pat while her gaze dropped to study Josie's ample abdomen. "We'll be looking forward to meeting your new arrival when we come back in July."

"Uh, yes." Josie was floundering and she knew it. Usually she was quite good at remembering her guests' plans, but she only vaguely remembered the Jensens having made another reservation to stay during the summer.

"Our family reunion, don't you know?" Mrs. Jensen said cheerfully. "All three of our daughters and their families. Lizzie had a baby at Christmas, so Ashley will be just a few months older than yours. You can compare notes. Your Sam can compare notes with her Mark, too. When Ashley was born, Mark fainted. I bet your Sam won't."

Josie didn't even venture a reply to that.

She just smiled her best cheery-innkeeper smile and prayed the Jensens would leave while she still had a little of her sanity intact.

"Why did you tell them you were my husband?"

Sam, who was standing on the front porch, waving goodbye to the third set of guests he had convinced that he was her spouse, stepped back at the ferocity in her tone.

"I didn't."

"No? You didn't say anything about having my rings resized?"

"Well, one lady said something about your not having any and she didn't give me the impression of someone who would approve of us living together."

"We don't live together!"

"We do now."

Josie's teeth came together with a snap. "You know what I mean. And I would appreciate it if you wouldn't mislead the guests. Especially not ones who will be back in three months expecting to see us all together as one big happy family."

Sam shrugged. "No big deal. I hope we will be."

"What?"

"You heard me."

Josie shivered involuntarily. "I told you no."

"That was yesterday."

"Nothing's changed."

"Yet."

Damn it. Why did he have to stand there and look so smug? So confident? So strong? So handsome?

"I won't change my mind."

He smiled. "Then I'll have to change it for you."

She shook her head. "You can't. You'll be in New York."

"No."

"What do you mean, no?"

"I'm staying here."

"You can't! You have a job! You're president of Fletcher's, for heaven's sake! People depend on you."

He looked straight at her. "There's only one person I want depending on me." Their eyes met, then his dropped and he looked at her belly. "One," he repeated, "for the moment."

"Don't be ridiculous!"

"I'm not."

"You can't stay here!"

"I *am* staying here, Josie," he said. "Get used to it."

He didn't mean it, of course.

He couldn't possibly. How could he run a multi-million-dollar New York based corporation from an inn on a bluff in Dubuque, Iowa?

He couldn't, Josie decided. And she breathed easier—until that afternoon when a man came to hook up the extra phone and fax lines.

"Where do you want 'em, miss?" the technician asked her over the top of a huge box he was struggling to hang on to.

She stared at him, nonplussed, then heard Sam's footfall behind her.

"Just bring them right up here. I'm setting up shop in Coleman's Room," he told Josie as he ushered the technician in.

"You can't! I've rented it," Josie protested.

"Too bad. Give them another room. Send them to The Taylor House."

"I'm not sending them to The Taylor House."

He shrugged equably. "Give them the love seat."

"I'll give them Mrs. Shields' Room," she said through her teeth.

"They'll like that. It's bigger. Better." Sam pointed the technician up the staircase to Coleman's Room. Then he turned back to Josie, who was staring at him in open-mouthed dismay. "Don't fuss," he said. "It's not good for you. Or the baby."

Josie wondered how he'd like a lamp right between the eyes.

Then she raised her eyes to heaven, though she thought she might do better sending this particular question in the other direction. "How could you, Hattie?" she asked her dearly departed friend and employer. "You don't know what you've done."

Sam was not an easy man to ignore. It would have helped if he'd stayed in Coleman's Room. But he didn't.

He kept popping into the kitchen, asking questions, scribbling notes, telling her to remind him about meetings with Thai businessmen and German watchmakers, or asking her to call his assistant, Elinor, and have her take care of the shipment of Japanese umbrellas.

Umbrellas, for heaven's sake!

Josie wanted to tell him to go jump in the lake. But she didn't want him to know he was rattling her.

It would have helped, too, if he hadn't decided to play innkeeper. Twice the doorbell rang, and when Josie was slow getting to it Sam was there before her, to greet the guests and show them around with the cheerful aplomb that made him such a successful businessman.

Josie told herself it was his right. He was her boss. She just wished he would say so.

Instead he always said, "This is Josie." Not, *This is Josie, the innkeeper.* Just, "This is Josie."

And then he'd look at her possessively, and all the women would take in Josie's protruding abdomen and Sam's doting expression, and they'd coo and smile and ask her when the baby was due and say wasn't it nice her husband was around all the time.

Josie wanted to strangle him. She wanted to wear one of those T-shirts that pointed at the man next to her and proclaimed HE'S NOT MY HUSBAND. She didn't dare.

We're not married, she wanted to yell at them. She didn't, because innkeepers didn't yell at guests.

She might, however, yell at her boss the next time she had a chance. Mostly she smiled politely, then made her escape. If he wanted to greet the guests, it was fine with her, she thought grumpily. It saved her from having to smile all the time.

"Look like you been suckin' a lemon. Don't she, Ben?"

Josie looked up from the wreath she was making for one of the rooms to see Cletus and Benjamin coming in the back door. She did muster a smile for the two old men, then dragged a hand through her hair.

The day had turned warm, and since she'd been pregnant she felt the heat more than usual and became grumpy. It was probably a good thing Sam had taken care of the guests. He'd be far more charming than she was at the moment.

It would be all she could do to muster enough equanimity to chat with Benjamin and Cletus. She knew they'd worried about her since Hattie died. She supposed they'd shared their worries with Sam.

Maybe, if she tried, she could get them to assure him she was fine. She clipped several small pieces of eucalyptus together and wired them to the frame, then looked up again and made an effort to broaden her smile.

"No lemons," she said. "I'm just hot."

"Want the air conditioning on?" Cletus asked.

"No. I'll live."

"Glad to hear it," Benjamin said dryly. "You don't sound 'specially thrilled."

Josie shrugged. "I'm feeling a little...out of sorts. That's all."

"Sam ain't draggin' his feet 'bout the weddin'?"

Josie's head jerked up. "What wedding?"

"Yours."

"There isn't going to be a wedding," Josie told them.

"Whatdya mean, there ain't gonna be a wedding?" Benjamin's snow-white brows drew down. "Course there is. It's why he come."

"It may be why he came, but that doesn't mean I'm going to marry him."

Cletus looked affronted. "Why not?"

"Because I don't want to," Josie said firmly.

"Why not?" demanded Benjamin.

Josie smothered a sigh. Where, she wondered, was it written that she had to explain her every decision to a couple of nosy old men?

"You don't get married just because you're going to have a baby."

"Sounds like a damn fine reason to me," Cletus huffed.

"Damn fine," Benjamin echoed.

Josie shook her head. "Not in my book."

"You got a better one?"

"Love."

"You do love him." Both of them looked at her then, challenging her to deny it.

Josie averted her eyes. She chewed on her lip. She wrapped some more pieces of eucalyptus and strangled them with the wire.

"Don't you?" Benjamin probed.

"Once I had a crush on him," Josie conceded with considerable irritation. "A long time ago."

Two pairs of brows lifted skeptically. Josie supposed she ought to be grateful they didn't point out that she hadn't gone to bed with him all that long ago. "It's over," she insisted.

Cletus cocked his head. "You don't still, um, got the crush?"

"No, I do not have the crush." It was only the truth. She'd gone far past "crush" years ago. She looked at them hopefully. "Do you suppose you could stay out of this?" she suggested.

"We was only tryin' to help," Cletus told her.

Josie mustered her patience. "I know that. But it isn't helping. It's making things harder."

"I'll marry you," Benjamin said.

Both Cletus and Josie stared at him, mouths agape.

"I will," Benjamin said, coloring to the roots of his hair. "I mean, if you're lookin' for someone who loves ya..." Pale blue eyes stared defiantly into hers.

Josie's heart melted. She dropped the eucalyptus and the wire and crossed the room to put her arms around Benjamin. It was a clumsy hug, made awkward by the child who burgeoned between them. But it was no less heartfelt for being so. "Oh, Ben." Josie kissed his ruddy cheek. "You are so good to me."

"I mean it," he said, shifting uncomfortably from one foot to the other. "I do."

"I appreciate the offer. You know I do. And I love you, too. Both of you." Her smile included Cletus. "But not the way I want to feel about the man I marry. And not," she added wistfully, "the way I want him to feel about me."

"You don't reckon Sam feels that way?" Cletus asked after a moment.

Josie shook her head. "No. It was a...mistake. We made a mistake. To marry him would be to make another one." She looked from one of them to the other, seeking their agreement.

Both men just looked at her and shook their heads.

She didn't know what she wanted. For one of them to talk her out of it, perhaps? For them to tell her that their night of love had not been a mistake? That Sam loved her the way she had always loved him?

But even if they had, it wouldn't have done any good. She would have to hear it from Sam himself to believe it.

And Sam would never give her words of love. Sam would only talk about duty and responsibility.

Josie didn't want to be just another of Sam's responsibilities.

She wished he'd go away.

And if he wouldn't of his own accord—well, she'd just have to see about helping him!

CHAPTER FIVE

IT SHOULDN'T have been so hard.

Sam was used to running his business by phone and fax. He was used to using E-mail and telexes to get things done. And if his Thai businessmen balked at coming to Dubuque, that was just too damn bad. He'd get by without them.

But nothing was going right. Nothing at all.

Messages got lost or garbled or mislaid. His desk got cleared and the trash emptied if he so much as stepped out to the bathroom. Projects he'd been working on for months simply vanished into thin air.

The new phone line kept disconnecting. The technician said he didn't understand what the problem was, but he came out and checked it. Everything looked fine to him. The line behaved perfectly—for him.

Sam wondered what inanimate objects had against him.

He asked Josie if she had the same problem on the inn's lines. She said no. It was almost the only thing she said to him.

She seemed to avoid him half the time, and the other half she was right where *he* needed to be, vacuuming or hammering or taking guests on tours of the room.

He'd always had a sort of vaguely romantic fantasy about how mellow and calm and, well, bovine, pregnant women were. Josie was neither mellow nor calm. And he didn't dare speculate on her bovine qualities—at least not within her hearing.

In any case, after three days, she was wearing him out. She couldn't just be pregnant and run an inn like a normal person. Not Josie!

She had to be pregnant, run an inn and simultaneously tackle six different remodeling and redecorating jobs.

One afternoon he found her hanging pictures she'd bought at a recent estate auction. Lugging and stretching and lifting. Then straightening and standing back and contemplating. Then taking them down and moving to another room and going through the whole process again. Mostly in rooms where he'd gone to escape and get some work done.

"You were in here already," he reminded her when she trundled into the library with a great monstrous frame filled with photos of early Dubuque buildings.

"I know. I thought I might find a better place." She shrugged. "I didn't." Her face was red from the exertion. She started to lift it again.

"Damn it! Give me that." Sam snatched it out of her hands. "Where do you want it?"

"There." She pointed at the wall above the old built-in cherry wood bookcases. He hoisted the cumbersome thing. "No, there." And she turned the other way and pointed to a spot above the brand-new built-in two-person whirlpool tub. "It'll give them something to look at while they're bathing."

Sam lowered the frame and carried it across the room. He set it on the edge, kicked off his loafers and climbed into the tub. "It's not what I'd be looking at if I was sharing this," he said over his shoulder.

Her already alarmingly red color deepened. "Just hang it," she said shortly.

Sam hung it.

"It's tilting to the left," Josie said. He adjusted it.

"Too much." He moved it back. "More." He moved it again. "There. Just right." She paused, contemplating it. "Maybe it would look better over the bookcases."

Sam got out of the tub. "Sorry, sweetheart. It's staying there."

"But—"

He turned on her. "Read my lips. It's fine."

"Then I'll move it." Josie started toward it.

Sam moved between her and the picture. But before he could head her off, he was interrupted by the shrilling of the phone.

It was Elinor. She was trying to get a shipment of Indian textiles through Customs. She needed some paperwork she had faxed to Sam to sign.

"I have to go upstairs and get them."

They weren't there. His desk had been cleaned again. His trash had been emptied. The papers were nowhere to be found.

Out in the hall he could hear Josie, vacuuming.

She was trying to get rid of him.

It didn't take a genius to figure it out. Even a man could figure that much. Sam dug in his heels.

"What in bloody hell do you think you're doing?" he demanded the next day when he came back to Coleman's Room after breakfast, shuffling through a stack of faxes on a missing shipment of jade, only to bump up against a ladder right inside the door.

Josie was on top of it. She arched around so she could peer down at him past her enormous belly. "Peeling off wallpaper. What does it look like?"

Sam glowered up at her. "Like you're trying to kill yourself. Get down."

"No." And she turned her back and continued to pull at the strip.

No?

No?

Sam felt as if his tie was choking him to death. He reached up to loosen it—remembered he was wearing a T-shirt. He dropped the wad of faxes on the floor, reached up and grabbed Josie by the hips, lifting her off the ladder.

"How dare you?" The second her feet hit the floor, she whirled on him, spitting fire.

"How dare I not when you're doing something as stupid as that?"

"It's my job! 'The innkeeper is responsible for upkeep.' Read my job description."

"I'll do better than that. I'll change your damn job description. Now stay off the ladder!"

"But I have to get it done. It's on my list. Hattie and I made a list over the winter—which rooms to paper, which rooms to paint. Paint fumes are bad for the baby, but wallpaper is fine. I've stripped wallpaper a dozen times. More. Who do you think did all this wallpapering?"

She was struggling against the hold he had on her as she babbled. But Sam wasn't letting go. He shifted his grip from her hips—the feel of which kept him from making a level-headed reply—to her wrists, which were only marginally less tempting.

"You did. But you weren't pregnant when you did them." Pause. "Were you?"

At last Josie managed to snatch her hands out of his grasp. "You know damned well I wasn't!"

"Well, you are now. With my child. So you'll damned well stay off the ladder."

She looked away. Impasse. She backed up and then allowed herself to glower at him. "It needs to be done."

"Then we'll hire someone to do it."

"Money solves everything? Is that it, Sam?"

His jaw tightened. He knew she was trying to goad him. Josie knew money didn't matter to him one way or another. But she didn't care about that. She only cared about keeping up a fight.

Did stubborn irrationality go with being pregnant? He didn't suppose it would be tactful to ask.

"Money will solve this," he said as calmly as he could. "Call someone and get him up here to do the stripping."

"Him?" Josie said scornfully. "How sexist is that?"

Sam ground his teeth. "Fine. Get a her. Get a set of identical triplets or a two-headed hyena! I don't care! Just stay the hell off the ladder!"

Josie glared. He glared back.

His phone rang. He ground his teeth, but didn't answer it. "I'm going to take this call down in the library," he said, holding up a hand to forestall her protest. "I don't care if it's rented tonight. They can damned well wait. Or they can go somewhere else. I have work to do and I'm going to do it. Here. And you're not going to stop me. The only thing you're going to stop is standing on ladders!"

Another shrill ring punctuated his words.

"Somebody gonna answer that phone?" Cletus hollered.

Sam punched the button of his portable and barked, "Fletcher. Hold on." He hit the hold button and fixed her with a hard glare. "Got it?"

For a full thirty seconds neither of them spoke. Then, "I'll get someone who needs the work," Josie said. Lifting her chin, she brushed past him out of the room and down the stairs.

From the back there was nothing pregnant about her. She looked just as she always had—like a very sexy woman with the world's longest, loveliest legs. Only the gentle roll in her movements betrayed the changes in her body. But—he swallowed—she still had the sexiest damn walk he'd ever seen.

He groaned.

The phone's hold light kept flashing. The fax number rang.

"Ain't anybody gonna answer the phone around here?" Cletus yelled.

Sam ignored the fax and punched the button on the portable. "What?"

"About time," Elinor said testily. "Mr. Rajchakit would like to speak with you. He's waiting. This is a conference call."

"Ah…" Sam mustered his smattering of Thai from the four winds. *"Sa-waht! Dee Krahp, Mr. Rajchakit."*

There was no time to think about Josie's legs now.

It wasn't the most productive week of his life, that was for sure.

He did—with about a thousand dollars' worth of phone calls—track down the jade shipment that he could have simply discovered on his own if he'd been in New York. He did get the cadre of Hong Kong businessmen, who had expected to see him next week, rescheduled for next month. He even got Mr. Rajchakit pacified with an agreement that they would meet in New York in two weeks' time. Sam wasn't sure he could make that meeting, either.

It depended on how quickly Josie came to her senses. Or how successful she was at driving him away.

He didn't want to admit it, but she was doing a pretty good job.

It was clear as Waterford crystal that she didn't want him here and was doing her best to make sure he left. There was continual noise and furore wherever he was, yet somehow she managed to keep a serene ambience for the guests.

While he was knee-deep in wallpaper, dust and fresh paint, everyone else seemed to be treated to a haven of tranquility. He didn't understand how Josie could provide peace and calm for them and produce a tornado of activity wherever he was trying to get some work done—but she did.

It took him five days to find his first bit of respite. He thought it was because he'd fooled her, sneaking into the Captain's Quarters to do some work.

He knew the room was rented that night, but he'd taken the call that said the guests—a honeymooning couple—wouldn't be arriving until late.

Great, he thought, and he barricaded himself in there without telling Josie.

He spent three hours in perfect solitude and caught up on the paperwork Elinor had faxed him. He even managed to make a few uninterrupted phone calls. No one put scaffolding over his head or painted around his chair or handed him a cat to hold.

At six, he felt as if he had conquered Everest. He swept the last piece of paper off his desk, then stood up and stretched mightily.

His back ached from having been bent over his desk so long. "You're out of shape," he chided himself. He picked up the papers, checked the room to make sure it was ready for the incoming guests, and then let himself out into the hall.

The whole house was quiet. In Mrs. Shields' and Mr. Shields' Rooms he could hear the soft murmur of already arrived guests. A couple were sitting in the Rose Parlor sipping sherry and reading the newspaper. Sam expected Josie to be there, pointing out church steeples and spouting off about local history. But she wasn't there. Errol Flynn was curled up under the fern stand. In the curved window overlooking the porch and the city, he saw Wallace Beery peering out. The cat turned his head when Sam came in.

"Where's Josie?" Sam asked him.

Wallace yawned.

The doorbell rang. Sam didn't answer it.

He had been told in no uncertain terms that it wasn't his job. It wasn't necessary. So he scratched Wallace's ears and was rewarded with a purr of contentment.

The doorbell rang again.

Sam waited, expecting to hear Josie's footsteps coming from the kitchen. The couple in the Rose Parlor looked at him expectantly. He frowned and poked his head in the butler's pantry. "Josie?"

He went on through the pantry to the kitchen. No one was there. He could see Cletus out back, watering flats of bedding plants. Josie wasn't with him.

Sam started to go back to answer the door. Benjamin was there before him, ushering the guests in.

"—not as quick as I used to be," he was apologizing to the two ladies who had been ringing the bell. "Shoulda been here to meet you. Live just down the way." He jerked his head toward the little house down the bluff. "Let me take those suitcases for you. This here's Sam," he said with another jerk of his head as they passed. "That there's Wallace Beery."

Sam smiled. Wallace purred. Benjamin ushered the guests up the steps.

It was an improvement, Sam thought. When Benjamin introduced him, he got top billing over the cat.

"Where's Josie?"

"She asked me to see to the place for a while," Benjamin said over his shoulder. "Right this way, ladies."

Benjamin did host duties the rest of the evening. Josie didn't show up for dinner, either. Sam wondered if she had gone out.

She hadn't had a day off since he'd been here, and of course she had a right to one, but she could have told him, he thought, nettled.

He fixed a meal for himself and Benjamin, hoping that the normally loquacious Benjamin would tell him where Josie had gone.

But, as far as Josie went, Benjamin had nothing to say.

He told stories about when he and Walter had plied the boat up and down the Mississippi. It sounded idyllic to Sam. A Tom Sawyer and Huck Finn sort of life. Tempting.

Sam remembered when Walter had still been alive, and they'd gone out on the river in his small boat to one of the islands where they'd cooked over an open fire and told stories far into the night.

Josie had been there, that night, her eyes bright, her face smiling, eager to hear the next outrageous tale. He could remember watching her, amused at her avid expression and her enthusiasm. She'd wanted to try rafting herself after that, and she'd set to making one the next day.

Sam had thought she'd give up after a few hours. He'd been wrong.

It had taken her three days to cut the wood and fit it together, working stubbornly all the while. He remembered when she'd taken it out for its maiden voyage—how radiant she'd looked, how supremely satisfied that she'd done it. She'd been dirty and mosquito-bitten and sunburned, and he didn't think he'd ever seen anyone with a wider smile.

He thought he remembered catching a glimpse of that smile the night they'd made love.

After Benjamin left, Sam sat in the parlor by himself, looking out across the city and the river, and thought about those times—and that night—and Josie.

He'd rarely let himself think about her since the night he'd slept with her.

It had seemed smarter not to dwell on it. There had been no point—she was Kurt's, not his.

But now?

She wasn't Kurt's any longer.

She wasn't his, either.

Still, this woman he barely knew—except for her stubbornness and her kindness to strangers and her smile—was going to be the mother of his child.

And he didn't have any idea where she was! Or who she was with. He raked his fingers through his hair and paced the length of the parlor. Damn her!

Nine turned to ten. Ten turned to eleven. No Josie.

He was wearing a hole in the rug with his prowling. Had she gone out with one of her friends? With Kurt?

The thought made him quicken his pace. He stopped by the phone, stared at it, then snatched up the phone book and looked for Kurt's number. He punched it in, wondering what he'd say if she answered. No one answered. Only an answering machine.

"This is Kurt Masters. I'm out for the evening. Please leave a message at the tone."

Sam slammed the phone down.

Out for the evening? With Josie?

Damn it, he wanted to know!

The doorbell rang.

He let the late arrivals in. It was the honeymooners who were going to stay in the Captain's Quarters.

"Hope you weren't waiting up just for us," the bride said, smiling.

Sam shook his head. "No." Despite his worry, the sight of them made him smile. The bride was still in her wedding dress, holding a layer of cake, and the groom in his tux had a pizza box in his hands.

"We didn't get to eat at the reception," the bride explained. "Hope you don't mind."

Bemused, Sam shook his head. He showed them to their room, gave them his best wishes and hoped that the traditional bottle of champagne Josie always left cooling in the ice bucket on the desk would go well with their pizza.

Then he noticed the champagne wasn't there.

He frowned. It wasn't like her to forget something like that. He'd expected she'd come in after he left. Obviously she hadn't. "I'll be right back. Newlyweds are supposed to get a bottle of champagne."

The bride, sitting cross-legged in the middle of the bed, tearing off a slice of pepperoni pizza, beamed at him.

The groom said, "I don't suppose you could make that a couple of beers?"

"Sure," Sam said. "Whatever you want."

He took the stairs two at a time down to the refrigerator, where he grabbed an entire six-pack and went back. "Here you go. Anything else you need, let us know."

"We won't need anything else," the bride assured him. She smiled at her groom.

He smiled back.

They both looked at the whirlpool bath and then the bed.

"Right," Sam said. He let himself out and shut the door.

Where the hell was Josie?

He knocked on her door. There was no response. But he saw a sliver of light beneath the door. Had she been here all the time?

"Josie?"

Nothing. He waited. "Josie." He allowed his voice to sound firmer this time.

Finally he heard the soft sound of footsteps. The lock clicked. The door opened.

Sam stared at the sight of her. *"What's the matter with you?"*

"Nothing."

It was clearly a lie. Josie looked as terrible as he'd ever seen her. Her face was ashen, her lips a dark smudge against the whiteness around them, her eyes like burnt holes.

He pushed open the door and brushed past her into her small sitting room. "What's wrong?"

She was wearing a robe and nightgown, the same ones she'd worn the night he'd taken her to his room, and they barely seemed to cover her abdomen. She hugged her arms across her breasts and shrugged awkwardly. "It's just…contractions."

"Contractions? Now? You're having the baby *now*?"

"No. Of course not." She shrugged. "At least…I hope not." The last three words were not spoken so much as breathed. She started to shake.

Sam cursed and put his arm around her, urging her toward the bedroom. "You need to be in bed."

"I was in bed."

"Sorry. Why the hell didn't you say?" He was practically shoving her now, trying to get her back there before she had the baby in the hall.

She didn't answer. She tried to shrug him off, but he wasn't being shrugged. He stayed right with her, pulling back the duvet and lifting her feet for her once she sat down, then tucking the duvet around her.

"Did you call the doctor?"

"Not this time."

"What do you mean, not *this* time? How the hell often does it happen?"

"Don't swear," she said wearily. "The baby can hear you."

"Babies react to tone of voice, not words." He didn't know if that was true, but it sounded plausible. "Call the doctor."

"There's no point. He'll just tell me to lie down. I've been lying down." She looked as white as the sheet on which she lay.

"When did they start?"

"About lunchtime."

"Lunchtime!"

"Not regularly," she said quickly. "Well, not very regularly." She turned her head away from him. Her fingers plucked at the duvet. "I just need to rest." Her voice was reedy, not firm. He saw her swallow. She wouldn't look at him.

"I'm calling the doctor."

She started to sit up. "You don't need—"

"I do need. I don't even know your doctor! I've never met him. Or her," he added after a moment, recalling their conversation about the wallpaperer.

"Him," Josie admitted gruffly.

"What's his name?"

For a minute he didn't think she was going to tell him. He wondered if he'd have to resort to shaking it out of her.

"Dr. Bastrop," she said reluctantly. "But you shouldn't be bothering him. Really. It's a Saturday night."

"Do all babies come nine-to-five Monday through Friday in your world?" Sam found the number in the phone book and was punching it in as he spoke.

"He won't be able to do anything! He'll just say I should go to bed and rest."

"We'll see," Sam said. Then, "This is Sam Fletcher. Get me Dr. Bastrop. At once."

Five minutes, one answering service operator and a doctor later, they were on their way to the hospital.

Josie could see why Sam was a successful CEO. Without raising his voice, without leaning on anyone, he bent the entire medical establishment to his will.

If *she* had called Dr. Bastrop's answering service, she'd have got a call-back. Then she would have been soothed, her fears would have been minimized, her desperation treated lightly. And that would have been the end of it.

Sam got action.

"Let's go," he said as he hung up and pulled the duvet off her. "We're going to the hospital."

Josie didn't move. She huddled in the bed, her arms wrapped around her. A contraction was squeezing her abdomen and she shook her head quickly. "No."

"Don't be ridiculous. The doctor's on his way. He's meeting us there."

Still Josie didn't move. She breathed lightly, shallowly, and tried to will it away. Something in her very stillness must have communicated itself to Sam. Suddenly he cursed again and hunkered down beside her.

"You're having one now." It wasn't a question. "Bad?"

She gave a quick negative shake and sniffled. "I don't think so. They don't hurt really. It's just—just—" She tried to sound calm. She didn't manage it. By the last few words, she reached a wail. "I don't know! What if it's coming? It's too early!"

"Which is why we have to get you to the hospital." He was so close she could feel his breath against her arm, his gaze intent on her. "Is it easing up? Can you sit up?"

She nodded shakily.

"Come on, then." Next thing she knew he had an arm around her and was raising her to a sitting position. Then he slipped his other arm beneath her knees. "I'll carry you."

Josie sat bolt-upright. "You won't carry me!" She dragged her robe around herself tightly. "Get out of here."

"You've got to go to the hospital, Josie."

"Then I'll go to the hospital. But I'm walking in under my own power. And I'm getting dressed first, so just get out of here so I can!"

He hesitated. She thought he might fling some comment at her about having seen all she had to offer already. But finally he nodded. "I'll wait right outside the door."

He went out and shut it behind him. His footsteps didn't move away, so she imagined he was being as good as his word.

As soon as the door was firmly shut, she got shakily to her feet and began to dress. A contraction stopped her in the middle of pulling on a sweater. It was stronger than the others, and she bent over, scared to death.

It would solve a lot of her problems, she knew, if she lost this baby. But she didn't want to lose it! That was the one thing she'd known from the moment she'd learned she was pregnant. She stayed huddled and bent until the contraction passed.

"Josie?" Sam's voice was quiet, but persistent on the far side of the door.

"Wait." She finished pulling on the sweater.

"Ready?" Sam said just as she sat down to put on her sandals. And whether she was or not didn't seem to matter. He opened the door.

"Here. I'll do that." And before she realized it, he was kneeling in front of her, slipping her feet into her shoes.

His short sun-bleached hair brushed against her denim-clad knees as he bent to his task. She could feel his fingers as they fumbled with the buckles. But he was much better at it than she was at the moment.

"It's a luxury," she couldn't help saying, "having someone else put on my shoes."

He looked up at her, past her enormous belly. Their eyes met. She ventured a tiny smile. He smiled back.

It was the first time she could remember them smiling

at each other since he'd walked in the door a week ago. It was a silly thing to smile about. It made her want to cry. Furiously she blinked back tears.

"Come on." Sam slipped an arm around her and drew her to her feet. "Let's go."

"I have to call Benjamin. Someone has to cover the house and the phones."

"I already called him."

When they got to the door, Benjamin was coming up the steps. He looked as if he'd been sleeping. He hadn't combed his hair and his shirt was untucked as he burst in the door.

"You all right?" he asked Josie. Without even waiting for an answer, he fixed his gaze on Sam. "You don't let anything happen to her, hear?"

Sam nodded. "Loud and clear."

The doctor had beaten them to the hospital. He was waiting in the emergency room when they got there. A big man, with salt-and-pepper hair and a walrus mustache, he had an easy-going, bluff manner that Josie found comforting.

He smiled now. "Had to brighten up my Saturday night, didn't you?"

"I'm sorry," Josie babbled. "I'm sure it's nothing. It's just that he—he—" her gaze went to Sam, who still hadn't let go of her elbow "—he wanted to be sure."

Dr. Bastrop's gaze met Sam's. He knew Josie hadn't wanted to drag her baby's father into her pregnancy. He didn't approve, but he didn't say so. Now he seemed to be taking Sam's measure, looking him over, assessing him. Unblinking, Sam stared back.

Finally Dr. Bastrop nodded. "Well, let's just have a look then, shall we?"

Sam started to follow them into the examining room

but Dr. Bastrop glanced over his shoulder. "You can't help with this part. Go pace in the corridor. I'll call you when I know where we stand."

For a minute Josie thought Sam might argue. But then he nodded and stuffed his hands into his pockets. "I'll wait here."

It wasn't comfortable, but then little that went along with having a baby—besides the initial act—was, in Josie's opinion.

When he'd finished his examination and she was dressed again, she sat on the edge of the table and watched Dr. Bastrop's face, trying to read his expression.

He wasn't giving much away. "How far apart did you say they've been?"

She ran her tongue over her lips. "Sometimes only a minute. Sometimes five."

"Since this afternoon?" He tapped his fingers on the counter, looked at her, then down at his fingers again.

"Am I having it?" she asked him when she could wait no longer.

"I hope not. Get the father in here," he said to the nurse.

A second later Sam burst through the door. "Is she all right?"

"She's fine."

"And the baby? Is he coming? Now?"

"I don't know yet."

"Can't you tell?" Sam asked urgently.

"Eventually."

"But—"

"We have to wait." He gave them what Josie guessed was supposed to be a reassuring smile. "I think that if you just rest and take it easy, these contractions will stop. Early false contractions are more common in later pregnancies. I wouldn't be as concerned if this was your third or fourth—or even second—child. I'd say it was just part of the process. But for a first pregnancy, I don't know. Even if you do deliver now, the baby would have a pretty fair chance of surviving. Lots of babies born at seven months—and even earlier—do. But nature likes her full nine months. Fewer problems. Better odds. I'd like you to go as long as you can." His gaze moved from Josie to Sam and back again.

"So fine, I'll slow down," Josie said immediately. "That's what I said all along."

"Slowing down isn't going to do it," Dr. Bastrop said. "You're going to have to stop."

"Stop?"

"Stop," the doctor said firmly. "I don't know if you've been over-exerting lately or not, but something's definitely upsetting the applecart."

Josie felt Sam's gaze turn on her at the word "over-exerting," and the color surged in her cheeks. "I had work to do! I didn't mean…" Her voice died. "I wasn't trying…" She looked away, fighting tears.

"No matter what you were doing, Josie, you can't do it now. You have to take it easy," the doctor said firmly. "And that means no rushing. No lifting. No stairs."

"I live on the second floor!"

"We'll move her down," Sam said at the same time, and the look he gave her dared her to argue. "And she'll stop. She'll stay in bed for the rest of her pregnancy if that's what you tell her to do."

Josie glared at his high-handedness.

But Dr. Bastrop nodded, pleased. "Good. It's about time you had someone take care of you," he said to Josie.

"I can take care of myself!" she protested, then winced as a particularly powerful contraction surged through her abdomen.

Dr. Bastrop put his hand on her belly, leaving it there until the contraction began to ease.

"I know you can take care of yourself, Josie," he said when at last it had. "All along you've done what was right for this baby. I'm sure you'll continue. Just be glad your man is willing to help you."

He's not my man! Josie wanted to scream. *He's never been my man. He's just the father of my child!* She pressed her fists against her eyes and rocked back and forth.

"Take her home and put her to bed," Dr. Bastrop told Sam, man to man. "Pamper her." There was a pause. "And keep your fingers crossed."

CHAPTER SIX

"You can't just evict them!" Josie said as Sam left her sitting on a chair in the kitchen and strode off toward the library where he had decided she was going to spend the night. "They're our guests!"

"They'll understand," Sam said over his shoulder.

Josie started to rise to go after him, but at the sound of the chair's legs scraping on the floor he turned around, the expression on his face sufficient to nail her right where she was. Slowly, warily, she sat back down.

"That's better. Now stay there. Don't even think of moving until I get back. Watch her," he said to Benjamin. Then, turning back to Josie, he said, "I'll have a room for you in a few minutes."

She didn't doubt it. He hadn't said a word all the way home in the car, but she could almost hear the wheels spinning in his head. The minute he'd settled her in the kitchen, he'd headed for the library. That was when she'd realized what he intended to do—what he was at this very moment actually doing!

She shut her eyes and groaned.

Benjamin bent over her. "You got a pain? How come they didn't keep you if you got a pain?"

Josie managed a faint smile. "No pain. I'm just worried."

"About the baby?"

"About what Sam's doing."

"Doing what he should be doing," Benjamin said firmly. "Taking care of things. Of you."

Was this some sort of masculine conspiracy? she wondered. Did every male within a hundred miles think that the minute she became pregnant she needed watching over?

The door swung open. "They're gone," Sam said. "I'll just change the sheets."

"You woke them up?" Josie was horrified.

"I doubt if they were sleeping," Sam said dryly. He gave a wry grin. "Anyway, they understood. I promised them a weekend on the house and moved them to another room for tonight."

"We don't have any other rooms."

"I put them in yours."

"Mine?" She stared at him, aghast. Her quarters were plain and simple, austere almost, with none of the amenities that graced the guest rooms.

"I couldn't put them in Coleman's Room. Not with wallpaper glop all over it." Sam arched a brow at her. "I believe, Josie dear, that that's what's called being hoist by your own petard."

She felt like sticking her tongue out at him. Instead she let out an irritated sigh and turned her head away so she wouldn't have to see his damnably superior smile.

He didn't waste much time bestowing it anyway. "I'll be back for you in a few minutes."

"I don't need you coming back for me," she snapped. "I know where the library is." It was all the acquiescence he was going to get from her. She sank back into the chair again, pressing her hands against her belly as another contraction hit.

Sam saw it and got a pinched look around his mouth. "I'll hurry."

Logically, sensibly, Sam supposed he ought to hope she'd lose the baby. It would forever cut the tie between them, solve their problems, simplify their lives.

But the very thought sent a shaft of ice-cold panic right through him.

He'd barely let himself think beyond the moment since he'd found out she was going to have his child. He'd not lain awake planning for the future. He had no concept of the baby he'd fathered.

And yet, the moment he'd thought it might not live, he'd known he would move heaven and earth to make sure it did.

Evicting guests was the least of his worries. He'd happily throw the whole damn bunch out if it would help Josie carry their child.

It wouldn't. In fact it would upset her more. She loved the inn—loved innkeeping. The Shields House, by rights, should have been hers.

He'd make sure it was. But, right now, his first task was to make sure she stayed quiet and calm.

He picked up the few things that lay scattered around her bedroom, making it presentable for the couple he'd tossed out of the library. Then he grabbed her nightgown and robe and ferreted through her drawers for clean underwear for tomorrow, feeling uncomfortably like a voyeur.

Once he got the couple settled in Josie's room, he went back and did the bed in the library. He'd never made a bed up so fast in his life. It wasn't a great job. The corners weren't tucked with military precision. The feather tick wasn't fluffed to its full loft. He didn't care if she found fault as long as she stayed there.

He went back to the kitchen and was gratified to find her where he'd left her. "Bed's ready," he said. "How you doing?"

"All right." But he still thought she looked pale. She

started to lever herself out of the chair and he hurried to help her. He didn't know whether to be glad or not when she didn't shake him off.

"Still having contractions?" he asked as he walked with her toward the library.

She nodded, but didn't speak. He could tell she was making an effort to walk at a normal pace, but there was a momentary hesitation in her step. When they got to the library, she stopped and turned. "Thank you."

It was a dismissal, and he knew it.

"You're welcome." But he didn't leave. Instead he moved toward her and all she could do was back up— until they were both in the library. He shut the door.

"What are you doing?"

"Staying." The look she gave him over her shoulder was scathing. He ignored it. "I brought your nightgown down." He held it out to her.

She snatched it and started for the bathroom. He took a step after her and she turned. "Don't come with me," she said. "Don't."

There was a thread of panic in her voice that stopped him. He wanted to tell her not to be stupid, that he'd seen her naked. He certainly wasn't going to jump her bones tonight! But that was logical. Josie was beyond logic.

He nodded. She disappeared around the corner into to bathroom. When the door shut, he went and stood outside it.

He could hear the soft sounds of her moving around. Then, for a while, he didn't hear anything. *Are you all right?* he wanted ask. He held his tongue. Five minutes later—which seemed more like five years to him—she opened the door.

Mutely he took her arm and felt her stiffen. He steered

her back to the bed, then turned down the duvet so she could get underneath it.

When she was, she folded her hands together on top of it. "There," she said. "Satisfied? I'm all tucked in. Now good night."

He shut off the lamp. The room went dark, the only light spilling in from the half-moon visible through the curtains. "Night, Josie," he said quietly. Then instead of going out, he crossed the room and sat down in the rocking chair.

She sat up. "Sam!"

He cocked his head. "What?"

"What do you think you're doing?"

He gave an experimental rock with one foot. The chair squeaked. "What's it look like?"

"You're not staying!"

"Make me leave," he said equably.

She made a furious sound. "You know I can't."

"I know you can't."

She pounded her fist on the feather tick. "Damn you, Sam Fletcher. Why are you doing this?" She sounded as if she was going to cry.

He got up abruptly. "Oh, God, don't cry." It had almost killed him listening to her cry last time. And that had only been about Kurt.

"I'm not crying," she said fiercely. But her voice cracked as she said it, and on top of the duvet she pressed her hands tight against her belly.

Sam went over and sat on the edge of the bed, reaching out and taking one of her hands in his. She tried to pull away, but he hung on. "Don't, Josie. Please." Her hand was cold. So cold. He chafed it with his fingers, rubbed his thumb over her knuckles. She stopped trying to pull away from him at last, and he curved his hand around hers.

"I won't sleep if I leave," he told her. "I'll be worried about you."

"I'll be all right."

"I hope so. But I need to stay. To be sure."

She didn't answer him. A soft sound of misery came from the back of her throat.

"What about tomorrow?" she said plaintively after a moment. "I've got to fix breakfast at six."

"I'll take care of it."

"You can't cook breakfast for eighteen people."

"I can," Sam said. "And there will be nineteen. I'll bring you breakfast in bed." He smiled at her in the dark.

"Don't be ridiculous."

"I don't think I'm the one who's being ridiculous," he said softly. His thumb continued to rub against her fingers. "Don't worry about tomorrow, Josie. It'll be all right. We'll handle it."

"I can't handle anything! The doctor said!" It was almost a wail.

"You can tell me what to do," he offered. Then he grinned. "You'll like that."

She opened her mouth as if she was going to argue with him. But then she sighed and settled back against the pillows again. Beneath his hand he felt an odd tightening in her belly. Her whole body tensed then, and she drew a breath and held it, unmoving.

Sam frowned. "Is that it? A contraction?" He'd never felt one, had only an academic notion of what it meant.

Accustomed to always being able to control his own body, he had a hard time imagining what it must be like to have it subject to forces he had no power over. He wondered if Josie resented it. He wondered if she resented him.

How could she not?

In one night he had changed her life, ruined her engagement, destroyed her freedom. He had wanted her, needed her comfort, her touch, her loving. And in taking it he had sentenced her to an existence she could only regret.

He sat now watching her in the moonlight, sat holding her hand in his, feeling the increasing tautness in her distended belly, and he wondered what he could do to make things right, what he could do to give her back at least a part of the life she had lost.

She didn't remember falling asleep. But when she woke up, she wasn't in her own bed and it took a moment for her to recognize where she was—and why.

The morning panic which said it was light and she was late and she had to be out of bed and fixing breakfast *right now* broke over her. But an even greater panic that said she had to *lie still* or lose the baby kept her right where she was.

She was on her side in the middle of the queen-size bed, hugging a pillow. It was a practice she'd developed since the baby had got big enough that she felt as if her abdomen needed a little support. At least, she assured herself, that was the theory.

Some nights she dreamed the pillow was Sam.

Now she slid her hand between the pillow and her belly and rubbed it gently across her abdomen. The baby seemed to stir within at her touch, but no muscles contracted. Josie rubbed it again. She waited, barely daring to breathe. A minute. Two. She counted. She had fallen asleep counting, she remembered that now. Counting.

And holding Sam's hand.

After five minutes of counting without any contractions, she breathed more deeply, felt the worry ease, rolled onto her back—and saw Sam sound asleep in the rocking chair next to the bed.

He sprawled there, long jean-clad legs outstretched, shirttails dangling, one golden whisker-shadowed cheek pillowed against his hand. On the table next to the bed she saw a breakfast tray. Orange juice. Pancakes. Bacon. A fruit cup.

"Oh, Sam."

She didn't think she said the words aloud—only breathed them. But, however loudly she'd said them, it was enough that he blinked and his dark eyes came slowly open to settle right on her.

He shoved himself up. "How you doing?"

The gentle concern in his voice almost undid her. She cleared her throat, trying to sound as if she'd been awake and watching him for hours, wishing she had been, wishing he hadn't seen her fast asleep. "I'm fine." She started to ease herself to a sitting position. He almost leapt out of the chair.

"Let me help you."

She shook her head quickly and backed up against the headboard, tugging the duvet with her. She needed to get out of bed and use the bathroom, but she wouldn't as long as he was there. He'd seen entirely too much of her parading around in her nightgown!

He stood beside the bed and shifted from one foot to the other, still looking down at her. "No more contractions?"

She pressed her lips together and gave a tiny shake of her head. "No contractions." She managed a smile. "The crisis is past." She said the words lightly, hoping he would take the hint that she didn't need him hovering anymore and would leave.

He didn't budge. "I brought you some breakfast earlier. Figured you'd be awake by the time I got back from feeding the hordes. Guess you must've been worn out."

"Guess so," she said in a small voice. She was as surprised as he was that she had slept so long. It was past ten. She straightened. "Who's on the desk? People will be checking out."

"Benjamin's handling it. He came up early and gave me some help with breakfast, too. Cletus is coming in an hour. Don't worry. Everything's taken care of. These pancakes are cold and the bacon's seen better days. I'll bring you something else."

She hesitated, torn between letting him because she wanted him out of the room and not wanting him to do any more for her. "I can get up now," she said. "If you leave," she added pointedly.

"I'll leave," he said. "But I'll be right back."

"You don't have to hover."

He didn't reply, just looked at her. She raised her chin and tried to look brisk and competent. Difficult since she was wearing a nightgown and her hair was a mess.

"Five minutes," he said, "and I'll be back."

He was true to his word, giving her just enough time to use the bathroom and wash her face, brush her teeth and comb her hair, before he returned, bringing her a plate of scrambled eggs, toast, fruit and juice this time. He set the tray on the table next to the bed where she sat.

"Thank you," Josie said. She waited for him to leave again. He didn't. "You don't have to wait around."

"We need to talk."

She reached for a piece of the toast, taking a bite. "About what?"

"About last night."

"Last night is over. I'm fine. I just overdid it yesterday. I won't overdo it anymore," she promised.

"No," he said gravely, "you won't." He was leaning against the bookcase now, not quite looming over her, but still high enough so that she had to look up to see his face. When she did, she found it was serious, unsmiling.

Josie gave him her best bright smile, hoping to change that, to coax one out of him. Sam, serious, did not bode well. He didn't smile.

He shoved himself away from the bookcase and strode across the room, hands in the pockets of his jeans, his head bent. When he got to the fireplace, he slanted her a glance. "You told me the other day you wanted this baby."

It wasn't precisely a question. It was more of a challenge. Josie's chin jutted. "That's right."

"Then what you've been doing for the last few days wasn't very smart, was it?"

She felt her cheeks flush, but she bristled, too. "I didn't know that, did I? I'd never deliberately do something to hurt my child!"

"Our child."

Josie's jaw tightened. She looked away. She did not want to see those deep brown eyes boring into hers. She did not want to feel Sam looking at her and finding her wanting. God, what would she do if the baby had eyes like Sam's?

"I would never do anything to hurt this child," she said firmly. "You have to know that."

"Then why won't you do what's best for it?"

Her eyes narrowed. "What's that supposed to mean?"

He turned and faced her squarely. "Marry me."

"We've been through that already, Sam."

"And I didn't buy your answer then, either. You say you want this child, but you aren't taking care of it. You—"

"I beg your pardon!" She flung the toast on the plate in a fury. "How do you know what I do and don't do? You've been here—what? A week!"

"And I've seen you work yourself to the bone the whole time."

"I needed—"

"You don't need! You want! You want to be independent. You want to get rid of me. You want everything your own way. And you say that's taking care of your child? Loving your child? Don't make me laugh."

Josie had never seen Sam angry before. She pulled her knees up against her belly, as if they could somehow protect her from his onslaught. "You don't know what you're talking about."

"Don't I, though? I think I do. I think you need to stop reacting to me like you're some sort of silly high school girl and start acting like an adult."

Stung, Josie glared. "Silly high school girl?" She could barely get the words out. How dared he?

"Think about someone besides yourself for a change," he snapped. "This isn't about what you want anymore. It isn't about what I want! It's about what's best for the child. *Our* child! Yours and mine. The baby can't make those decisions. We have to. Both of us. Not just you."

"You're trying to. Bossing me around. Bullying."

He snorted. "Bullying?" He looked at her in bed,

then at the breakfast tray he'd brought her. His brow arched.

Josie knew what he was thinking: some bully. She hugged her knees and didn't look at him. She didn't answer him, either. She couldn't. It wasn't fair, she thought. None of it was fair.

She heard him come over to sit on the chair a few feet from the bed. Reluctantly she looked at him as he leaned forward, resting his elbows on his knees as he looked at her. His chocolate-brown eyes were dark and intent.

"Do you want this baby to survive?" he asked her.

"Of course I do!"

"Then you owe it its best chance. And you have to take it easy for that to happen. The doctor said so. He said you have to rest. Stay calm. Eat right. Sleep a lot. And you can't do that while you're playing innkeeper."

"I am not *playing* innkeeper!"

"You aren't giving the baby a fair chance if you don't back off."

"So I'll back off. I'll take it easier. That doesn't mean I have to marry you," she said tightly.

"It does if you want to keep your job."

She gaped at him. "You'd fire me?"

"Yes! No!" He raked a hand through his hair. "Hell, I don't know! No, I wouldn't fire you. But I want you to see sense. I want—" he sighed "—I want my child to have my name."

They stared at each other. Then she said softly, "Why?"

"Because he's mine! I want my child to have my name. I don't want him denied his birthright. He's a Fletcher, damn it!"

Josie stared, startled at his vehemence, at his insistence on wanting a child he'd never counted on. "Or she," she said after a moment.

"Or she," Sam amended. "Whichever. I don't care. I don't want to be on the outside looking in—"

"Like you'd know about that."

"I don't know much about that, you're right," he said. "For the most part I haven't ever had to do that. But you have. Did you like it?"

"Of course I didn't like it."

"Then why would you think I would? And why do you think our child will?"

"Our child won't! Our child will never go through what I went through! Our child will have a mother who loves it and cares for it all the days of her life!"

Sam nodded slowly. His gaze dropped for a moment, then lifted and bored into hers. "Good. I want our child to know a father's love, too."

The words were quiet, but the intensity behind them was clear.

"You don't want to stay married, we don't have to stay married," Sam said. "If you feel that strongly about it, after the baby's born, we'll get a divorce."

"What good will that do?" Josie demanded. She felt as if he was tearing her heart out. Marry him, then divorce him?

"It will make him—or her," Sam added before she could correct him, "legitimate. It will prove to him—or her—that I cared enough to want to make sure of that. And it will give me the right to have some say in his—or her—upbringing."

"I wasn't going to deny you that right."

"Then don't deny me the chance to be a lawful wedded husband and father. Please." He was so close she could see the muscle tic in his jaw, could remember the rough whiskery feel of it against her skin when they'd made love.

"I'll make it worth your while," he added when moments passed and she didn't speak.

"Worth my while?"

"Hattie should have given the inn to you, not to me. She would have if she hadn't wanted me to know about the child. Marry me and I'll see that it's yours."

Josie stared at him. "That's like marrying for money. I won't marry for money," she said firmly. "I'd never marry for money!"

Sam made an exasperated sound. "Then, don't. Marry me because it's the right thing to do. Marry me because you love our child."

Once upon a time Josie had daydreamed of marrying Sam.

When she'd been young and foolish and innocent, when she'd still believed that all things were possible, she'd indulged that dream. She'd lain awake at night and imagined Sam Fletcher asking her to marry him.

She'd envisioned him smiling at her, touching her gently, waiting hopefully. And when she'd said yes, she'd imagined the touch of his lips on hers.

It was a good thing she had her imagination. Reality was nothing like it.

"Think about it," he said. And then he left her there.

She thought about it. She thought that what he was urging was, if not exactly a business proposition, then something very like one. It was, as he said, the sensible, the logical, the proper thing to do. It was the best thing for their child.

Josie couldn't argue.

She wanted to. She tried to. She sat in the library long

after he'd left her and debated with herself. She thought of every argument, of every possible reason that he could be wrong.

But he wasn't wrong.

Ultimately she had to admit that marrying Sam was—for the sake of their child—the right thing to do.

CHAPTER SEVEN

IT WAS not going to be a hole-in-the-wall affair.

Five or ten or fifteen years down the road, when his child asked about their wedding, Sam wanted to be able to tell him—or her, he amended in deference to Josie, that they'd done things right.

Of course he got an argument from Josie.

"Your *mother?*" She was aghast after she told him she'd marry him and he told her his plans. "You want to send for your mother?" The color rose, then drained from her face.

"My mother would expect to be at my wedding," he said flatly. "So would my aunt Caroline and my aunt Grace and my uncle Lloyd. My cousins, too," he added. "Darcy and Catherine and Alexis."

"Why don't we just invite the whole town while we're at it?"

"Go ahead. You can invite as many or as few as you want," Sam said, ignoring her sarcasm. "Benjamin will come, of course. And Cletus. That goes without saying. Who else do you want?"

Josie's jaw was working. She turned away from him and stared blindly out the kitchen window. "Nobody! I don't want any of them! Why are you making such a big deal of this?"

"Because we're getting married." It seemed right. Appropriate. Important. As if they'd regret it later if they didn't.

"Some marriage," she snorted.

116

He shrugged. "It's the only marriage we've got."

Josie didn't look convinced, but she didn't argue anymore. She just turned her back and went on putting together a wreath for one of the rooms. It was something she could do sitting at the counter, so Sam didn't say anything more.

She was already annoyed enough at him because he had insisted she stay downstairs and take it easy all day. He knew she was only marrying him because her common sense told her she ought to. He knew she didn't love him.

Hell, after what he'd done to her, she probably didn't even like him anymore.

Well, too bad.

She could make the best of things, just as he was going to do.

He was making her call a caterer. And a florist. A cellist. And a baker. He wanted a meal. Flowers. Music. He wanted a *wedding cake!*

Josie told herself he was crazy. He couldn't really intend to make a big deal out of their wedding, could he?

Apparently he could. And was.

Within hours of her having agreed to become his wife, their wedding plans were off the ground. By nightfall she had an even greater appreciation for his ability to bend the world to his will. She didn't know what he told his mother or his uncle or his aunts about his precipitous marriage. She only knew his mother would be arriving on Wednesday.

"The rest will come on Friday. And we can get married Sunday night. Is that all right?" he asked her, as if her opinion mattered.

No, she wanted to scream. *No, it's not all right.*

But she'd made her decision to marry him. She given her agreement. She nodded her head.

She felt awkward and foolish all the same. She felt as if the caterer could see right through her fumbled explanations. She felt as if, all the time they talked about daffodils and daisies, the florist was shaking his head. But she drew a breath, steadied herself, and plowed on, doggedly making the arrangements Sam suggested.

And she knew that even though she was embarrassed, he was giving her memories.

Someday memories would be all she'd have left.

She tried not to think about that. She regained her equilibrium. She gave in, albeit not very gracefully, and allowed him to move her things into the library for the duration of her pregnancy. She dealt with the guests by smiling and chatting and not by racing up and down the steps fetching and carrying for them.

"See?" Sam said one afternoon after she'd just given a group of guests sightseeing directions without ever leaving her parlor chair. "Even you can be a lady of leisure." He grinned.

Josie stuck her tongue out at him.

What she wasn't going to be able to do, she was positive, was face his mother with any amount of poise.

How could she look Sam's mother in the eye and pretend that this was just another wedding?

"It's not 'just another wedding,'" Sam said when she asked him that. "It's ours. She won't be expecting you to be blasé."

"She'll hate me," Josie said. "She'll think I trapped you!"

"She was a little surprised," Sam admitted. "But she

understands all about passion. She was passionate about my dad.''

"It's not the same thing!"

"But she doesn't know that."

His reassurance did very little to assuage Josie's fears, though, for she was passionate about Sam. He just didn't know it. And he certainly wasn't passionate about her.

So she waited with trepidation for Sam to bring his mother back from the airport Wednesday afternoon. She'd debated going with him, wondering if getting it over with out at the airport might not be smarter. But in the end she chose to stay home because there would be guests arriving.

They had three couples coming in that afternoon. Sam had wanted her to call them and say that she'd made alternative arrangements for them. He'd wanted her to close the inn completely.

She had refused. "It's a business," she'd argued. "You can't close a business on a whim."

He'd looked as if he was going to argue with her. But then he'd clamped his mouth shut and given a jerky nod of the head. "Fine. Do what you want," he'd said through his teeth. "It'll be your inn soon enough."

That wasn't why she had insisted, no matter what he thought. But she hadn't said anything other than, "I'll wait here for them to arrive."

Sam had gone to get his mother alone.

Josie didn't know what he'd told her. Not the truth, she was certain.

If Sam had told her the truth, she was sure his mother wouldn't have smiled at her quite so warmly when he brought her in and introduced them. She tried to smile warmly in return, but she felt so huge and awkward and, what was worse, phony. Sam's mother ought to be meet-

ing a woman he loved when she got to meet his bride-
to-be. Not someone he'd got lumbered with because of
scruples and bad luck.

"This is Josie," Sam said. Then he smiled encour-
agingly at Josie. "This is my mother, Amelia."

Josie never had trouble meeting guests. It was one of
her gifts, making people feel at home. But she felt totally
tongue-tied and inept now.

"I'm so glad to meet you, Josie," Amelia said, taking
her hand and drawing her forward so she could lay a
soft kiss on Josie's heated cheek. Then, still holding her
future daughter-in-law's hand, she turned to Sam and
smiled. "Now I know what a Josephine Nolan is," she
said. "And I understand completely why Hattie left her
to you."

"My mother got the will first," Sam explained. "She
wondered."

I'll bet she did, Josie thought, wanting more and more
to sink through the floor. She was grateful at least that
when Amelia had said that she understood her gaze had
remained firmly on Josie's face instead of dropping to
her enormous belly. Sam had said his mother was pos-
sessed of exquisite tact. Josie believed him.

"Go phone your secretary or bother the customs office," Amelia said to Sam now, "and let me get ac-
quainted with Josie." When he hesitated, she made a
shooing motion with her hand. "Go on. I won't bite her.
I promise."

Josie managed her best resilient smile. "We'll be
fine," she assured him—and prayed it was the truth.

The truth was that Amelia was every bit the capable
dynamo that Sam was. She seemed to understand im-
plicitly that Josie was not a girl whose background one

inquired into too closely. But she didn't make her feel uncomfortable because of it.

She focused instead on the improvements Josie had made in the inn, allowing Josie to display her competence. And, once the younger woman was breathing a bit easier, she tackled the arrangements for the wedding.

Josie was glad she'd done a thorough job and could report exactly what the caterer would be serving and how, exactly what flowers were being used and where, exactly which musical pieces were being played and when, exactly what kind of cake she had ordered and how many layers. She thought she acquitted herself rather well.

Then Amelia said, "May I see your dress?"

"D-dress?" Josie choked on the word. The color drained from her face.

Amelia looked momentarily as dismayed as Josie did. But then a soft smile lit her face. "You forgot your dress." Just as if it was the most natural thing in the world!

How Freudian is that? Josie asked herself.

Where on earth would she ever find a wedding dress to fit an elephant? The answer was: she wouldn't. Subconsciously she must have known it and therefore had failed to even think about looking.

"I don't need anything special," she said quickly. "Nothing special would fit me. I'm hardly your average run-of-the-mill bride." She looked down at her burgeoning belly and then at Sam's mother with a wry smile.

"No bride is ever run-of-the-mill," Sam's mother said gently. "All brides are special. And every bride deserves a special dress."

*   *   *

It was the most beautiful dress Josie had ever seen.

And it was hers.

Made for her by Sam's incredibly talented mother in the few days they'd had left. Josie couldn't believe it. She'd had to pinch herself every time she looked at it hanging in the wardrobe in the library. She'd had to blink whenever she saw the reflection of herself wearing it in the mirror.

"There," Amelia said now, through a mouthful of pins. She was sitting on the floor looking up with enormous satisfaction at Josie, who stood mesmerized by the sight of herself in such a wondrous creation. "That'll do. Don't you think?"

"I think it's wonderful," Josie said—and meant every word. She'd been quite sure she'd end up being married in a flour sack or a pair of spandex maternity slacks and a smock. But Amelia had had other ideas.

"Josie and I are off to the fabric shop," she'd told Sam Wednesday afternoon.

He'd frowned. "Josie's supposed to be taking it easy."

"She will be," his mother had assured him. "I'm the one who's going to be doing all the work."

Josie hadn't believed it at the time. She'd gone along, bemused, while Amelia had speculated aloud about the sort of dress required.

"An Empire waistline, I think," Sam's mother had said. "How kind of Jane Austen to be all the rage just now. Yes, gathered right below the bosom. I can add extra fullness if we need it. And—" she'd turned to assess Josie's breasts "—a scoop-neck. Long sleeves or caps? Which do you prefer?"

"Um," Josie had said, who'd never considered the question.

"Long," Sam's mother had decided. "Unless I don't have time. Then we can do short."

Josie truly had been just along for the ride. Amelia had consulted her about color. "Ivory or white?" she'd asked as she held up bolts of satin against Josie's rosy skin.

"Ivory?" Josie had ventured. She didn't feel quite virginal enough for white.

"Ivory," Amelia had agreed briskly. She had given Josie an approving nod. "You have an eye for what will work."

So had Amelia, it was apparent. And a determination to bring it off.

"Can you really make me a wedding dress in three days?" Josie had asked her when they'd come back laden down with satin and lace and zippers and buttons and buoyed by Amelia's enthusiasm.

"Well, it won't be a designer dress," Amelia had said. "But it will do, I should think."

Now it was Sunday morning, and as she looked at the young woman standing in front of the mirror admiring herself in the Empire-waisted, scoop-necked ivory satin dress with the lace and satin bodice and the long lace sleeves, she waited for the verdict.

"Suit you?" she asked at last when Josie simply stared and turned and stared some more.

Josie could only smile and say, "Oh, yes."

Sam didn't know why he was so nervous. It was just a wedding after all. Just he and Josie doing what was necessary for the child they'd begotten. Important, yes, but hardly earth-shaking.

So why was he? Shaking, that is?

He held out his hands and studied the fine tremor in

his fingers. He reached up and eased a finger inside his shirt collar, hoping to find a bit more air. He wore a tie almost every day of his life and he'd never been strangled by one yet.

But this one—this one just might.

The cellist was playing something suitably serious that Sam recognized but didn't know the name of. Not the piece Josie was going to enter on, he knew that much. But he couldn't help lifting his eyes to the stairs as if she might already be there.

He hoped she would get down the stairs in one piece. Personally he didn't see why she didn't just walk into the parlor through the dining room and join him in front of the fireplace where the minister was standing now.

"She needs to make an entrance," his mother had insisted. "She'll come down the stairs."

"She's not supposed to go *up* the stairs," Sam had pointed out. "You're not," he'd said to Josie flatly in case she got the same stupid idea in her head that his mother had.

"She's not supposed to climb them," Amelia had agreed. "So you can carry her."

For an instant, Sam had gaped. But the same instant's flare of eagerness in Josie's eyes had made up his mind.

"Right," he'd said. And he strode across the room, swung her into his arms and carried her up then and there.

"You can't! I'm not—I'm not dressed!" Josie had protested.

Sam had stopped and looked down at her very proper trousers and smocked top. "You're not?" he'd said in his most hopeful lascivious tone. He'd been gratified when she almost smiled.

She'd punched his arm lightly. "You know what I mean. My dress."

"I'll bring your dress up," Amelia had said. "Sam's not supposed to see you in your dress until the wedding anyway."

Like this was a traditional wedding, Sam thought now, wiping damp palms down the sides of his black trousers.

And then the cellist stopped playing, and Benjamin appeared on the landing. He studied the assembled group below—Sam's relatives, a couple of friends of Josie's, the foster-parents she'd lived with before she'd come to stay at Hattie's—then looked at Sam. The murmuring stopped and a hush fell over the room. Benjamin nodded his head.

The cellist turned the page over and began to play.

Standing by the fireplace, Sam watched as Josie, one hand on Benjamin's arm, came slowly down the stairs, making the entrance his mother had promised.

She looked, Sam thought, like an angel descending from on high.

His throat constricted slightly as he stared at her. Exactly like an angel and an earth goddess combined, with her glorious motherly shape draped in soft yet elegant satin ivory, her arms encased in the finest lace, the tops of her wonderful breasts just barely peeking out from the scooped neck of the dress his mother had made her. Her long dark hair had been swept up away from her face and caught in a band of orange blossoms. Her face was flushed, her eyes dark and serious and unblinking as they zeroed in on him. She looked radiant. The way a bride ought to look.

If only she would smile.

He wanted her to smile.

He stepped forward almost before she reached the bottom of the stairs. He held out his arm to her before she'd even begun to relinquish Benjamin's. He heard someone murmur something and someone else titter.

He didn't notice. He didn't care. He saw only her.

He remembered the night he had gone to her room. He remembered her tear-streaked face. After that he remembered only bits and pieces. Touches and nibbles. Gentle caresses and urgent needs. But it was enough.

He remembered her kisses. He remembered her smile. *Smile,* he urged her silently now. *Smile for me.*

"Dearly beloved," the minister began, and out of the corner of his eye Sam saw the color drain from Josie's face. He felt her fingers clench against the fine wool of his coat. He reached over and rubbed his thumb over her fingers. They trembled until he curved his own around them tightly.

"Will you, Samuel, take Josephine...?"

The words flowed over him—love, cherish, honor, sustain. Richer, poorer. Sickness, health. As long as you both shall live—and then the minister was looking at him, waiting for him.

He said, "I will."

"Will you, Josephine, take Samuel to be your lawfully wedded husband...?"

He looked at his fingers wrapped over hers. He looked at her belly which was the reason they were here. He wondered what she heard in the words the minister was saying.

She said, "I will."

"Rings," said the minister.

Sam's head jerked up. So did Josie's. They stared at each other. No question now what she was thinking, Sam thought. Same thing he was thinking: *Omigod, I forgot the rings.*

He remembered lying to the guests about having Josie's rings resized. He'd never thought of it again. Cletus poked him in the side with an elbow. Once. Then again. Sam turned to glower at him. Cletus pressed a ring into his palm.

Sam stared at it. Cletus arched his brows expressively, then stepped on Sam's foot for good measure.

"With this ring, I thee wed," the minister intoned, and looked at him expectantly.

Sam fumbled the ring, then got it between his nerveless fingers and took Josie's hand in his.

He slid it on.

Josie looked at it, then up at him. "It's Hattie's ring," she said.

And then she smiled at him.

It was a good thing they had Benjamin and Cletus and Amelia, Josie thought. If she and Sam had been left to get married on their own, there was no telling the hash they might have made of it.

But with a little help from their friends—and Sam's relatives—the wedding had come off perfectly. There was even a ring for Sam.

Amelia had pressed a plain gold band into Josie's hand seconds before the minister looked at her expectantly. Later she found out it was the ring Amelia had given Sam's father.

"I hope you don't think I'm interfering," Amelia said afterward, during the reception. They'd finished the dinner the caterer had served—tender, buttery chicken Kiev with fresh asparagus and twice-baked potatoes—and were now listening to Sam's uncle toast the newly wedded couple with long-winded enthusiasm.

"Of course not," Josie said. She managed a smile for

the woman who was, for however short a time, her mother-in-law. She liked Amelia at lot. She wished she weren't going to lose her when she lost Sam.

"Sam would have had it eventually anyway," Amelia went on, "but it's lovely that he had it for his wedding. Unless," she amended, "you want to give him one of your own?"

"N-no." Josie shook her head. "It's fine."

It would be one less thing for him to give back to her when he left her.

She twisted the matching band and diamond solitaire on her own finger. She would have to be sure he got Hattie's ring back as well.

The thought of ending their marriage when they'd just begun it made her throat constrict. She blinked her eyes and turned away from Amelia, needing a moment to restore the smile she'd managed to keep on her face during most of the reception. Then she turned back, smile in place—and felt a contraction.

It caused the smile to falter again, just briefly.

She'd had a few contractions since the night Sam had taken her to the hospital. This was probably no more significant than those. Just the same, she put a surreptitious hand against her abdomen.

"Are you all right?" Sam's voice in her ear startled her.

She dropped her hand quickly and turned her head to give him a brilliant smile. "Of course."

His dark brown eyes searched hers for a long moment. Then he dropped his gaze to where their child curled beneath her satin-covered belly. "You'd tell me, wouldn't you, if you weren't?"

"Yes."

"—wish you many years of married happiness," Sam's uncle finished, raising his champagne glass.

Sam and Amelia and the rest of the guests drank deeply. Josie sipped her grape juice and wished Sam's uncle's wish would come true. She felt like an imposter, deceiving them all.

"Come along, dears," Amelia said. "Time to cut the cake."

Josie had another contraction while they were cutting the cake. She didn't think she called attention to it. She smiled gamely while Cletus's friend, Ambrose, took photos of them cutting the first piece, then taking turns feeding each other bites. She shivered at the touch of Sam's tongue against her fingers as he nibbled the piece of cake. She knew he didn't mean anything by it. It was just—

Happening again. This time it came from around the back, spreading and tightening, and Josie sucked in an involuntary breath. She dropped the cake she was feeding Sam. He retrieved it and tossed it onto a nearby plate.

"Let's try it again," Ambrose said, waving them back to stand behind the cake again.

But Sam shook his head. "Once is enough." His fingers sought Josie's. "Carry on with the party," he said to the assembled guests. "I'm taking my bride up to bed."

Josie went crimson as all the guests smiled and laughed.

"We can't leave now," she whispered at him under her breath.

"It's now and bed, or later and the hospital." He met her gaze levelly. "Take your pick."

Josie sighed and headed for the library, where she'd

slept since he'd brought her home from the hospital last time.

"Not there."

And, before she could say a word, he swung her up into his arms again and, parting the crowd, started up the stairs.

"Where are we going?" Josie demanded. "What are you doing?"

"Taking you on our honeymoon," Sam said.

"Honeymoon?' she squeaked.

"The Captain's Quarters." He waited until they were around the corner and on their way up to the third floor before he added, "It seemed appropriate somehow."

The Captain's Quarters. The room in which they'd made love. The room in which their child had been conceived.

It would have been a perfect place to go back to—if their wedding had been a love-match, if their marriage were going to be real!

Josie felt like crying. She stayed limp in Sam's arms until he reached the third floor. Then she struggled to get down. "We're here. You don't need to carry me."

He hesitated, looking down into her eyes for a moment. She hoped he didn't read her pain in them.

She tried to return his gaze equably, as if she were feeling calm and together and matter-of-fact. She must have done a good job for slowly he nodded and lowered her so that her feet touched the floor. But he didn't let her go as he opened the door.

Josie went in, eyes averted so she wouldn't have to look at the bed. She sat down in the rocking chair. "Thank you. I'm fine now. You can go back downstairs."

Sam just looked at her. "Not quite. I'm staying here. I meant what I said."

Josie stared up at him and swallowed, her eyes wide. "About what?"

"About taking you to bed."

CHAPTER EIGHT

IT WAS not the brightest idea Sam had ever had—taking Josie upstairs and proposing to spend the night with her.

It was, in fact, pretty stupid.

Perhaps he could put it down to the champagne his uncle Lloyd had been pouring so liberally. Or to the titters and blushes of his two maiden aunts. Or Benjamin and Cletus's high fives and winks. Or the tears he'd seen in his mother's eyes when she kissed him and Josie and told them how happy she was.

Or maybe it had been the sight of Josie herself, smiling bravely and standing tall, even when he could see that she was about to topple over any moment.

He'd felt a desperate need to gather her in his arms and protect her, to pick her up and carry her away with him.

So he did.

And once he was in the room with her, once he'd shut the door on the noise and revelry below, once he'd caught a glimpse of her long legs peeking out from beneath the ivory satin of her dress and of her flushed cheeks and fathomless eyes, he didn't want to go.

He leaned against the door and prayed she wouldn't throw him out.

Josie looked at him expectantly.

When he didn't move, he saw her swallow.

"Taking me to bed?" she asked warily after a moment.

He didn't say anything, staring down into the abyss

of decision, knowing even as he stared that the decision was already made.

"Why not? We're married," he said firmly. Then, "I can't leave, can I? What would they think? The groom can't just walk out and let the bride sleep alone on her wedding night."

"He can't?" Josie seemed to consider that a moment. Then she shrugged and looked up at him from where she sat on the bed. A small smile touched her lips. "I guess he can't."

Her words let Sam breathe again. But then she moved, her skirt hiked farther, and his breath caught in his throat. He shoved himself away from the door and took a step toward her. "So...since I'm staying, let me help you—" he cleared his throat which seemed suddenly tight "—out of your dress."

Josie stared at him, blinked, then looked down at her wedding gown. A deep rose color seemed to spread upward from her neckline.

"It's not like I—" Damn, his voice made him sound as if he was fourteen again! "I haven't, um, seen you before...um, without it, I mean."

"I...guess not." She raised her hands and held them out to him.

He ran his tongue over suddenly parched lips, then reached out and took her hands and pulled her to her knees on the bed. The satin tented out over her belly. Sam moved around behind her and worked loose the hook at the base of her neck. His fingers skimmed over her skin and he felt a shiver run through her. A similar one ran through him. A hungry one. A needy one. One he forced himself to suppress.

He eased the zipper down and bared her back to view. Then he slid the dress away from her shoulders, drew it down her arms. He stood so close behind her that the scent of her—a heady mixture of lilacs and something that hinted of citrus—tantalized him. He breathed it in, remembered a flash of how it had been to bury his face in her hair and have the aroma overwhelm him. He bent closer, breathed deeper.

She shivered and gave a tiny, self-conscious laugh. "It...tickles."

"What does?"

"You...um...breathing on me." She turned her head and slanted a glance up at him. There was the faintest hint of a smile on her face, as if she was afraid to really smile, as if she didn't know if she dared.

He'd got a smile out of her earlier when he'd slipped Hattie's ring on her finger. He wanted another now. He bent his head and nibbled at her ear.

"Sam!" She batted at him and tried to wriggle away.

He caught her at the waist with his hands, tickling her gently, and she squirmed, laughed, and toppled onto her side. He fell with her, holding her, drawing her close. His breath touched her neck, his lips followed.

She made a small sound in the back of her throat, a sound that made all his hormones stand at attention, that made his body press against hers. His hands splayed across the curve of her midsection. He felt it go hard, contract.

Josie stilled at once. So did he, hands still spread, unmoving, until at last he felt it ease. When it was over, she seemed to relax a little. She shifted her weight and turned slightly away from him, but she didn't pull away completely.

"A contraction," he said. It wasn't a question, but she nodded.

And then he felt something different. Not a tensing, a

thump—under his hand. He jerked back, frowning. "What's that?"

"The baby." There was the hint of a smile in her voice.

Sam swallowed. The baby? *Their baby?* Their baby *kicked?* He didn't know why he was so astonished. Surely he knew that babies moved. Kicked. But—kicked *him?*

"God," he breathed.

Josie turned her head. "Surprised?"

He nodded. "I'd never... I didn't think—" He felt foolish. "I'd never thought about it before. Does it... kick very often?"

"Sometimes I think it kicks all the time." She shrugged lightly. "That's not true, really. Sometimes, though, I think it's nocturnal." There was that smile again. "Kicks all night long."

"How do you sleep?" He pressed his hand flat against her belly and felt the tiny thumps.

"Some nights I don't."

She said it matter-of-factly. Not as a complaint. He hadn't heard Josie complain once—not about the baby he'd left her with, not about the inn that Hattie hadn't left her with, not about anything. He drew her back against him and pressed a kiss on her shoulder. Her skin was so soft and smooth. He wanted— He wanted—

He groaned and dragged himself away. "Let me help you out of that," he said gruffly, keeping his eyes averted.

It didn't matter what he wanted. He couldn't have it.

Awkwardly Josie got off the bed, and Sam helped her strip off the gown. He made sure his movements were perfunctory. He didn't let his fingers linger against her soft flesh. He didn't let his hand trail down the length of her spine to the hollow at its base. He tried not to touch more than necessary. He tried not to breathe at all.

Josie certainly did her part. She kept her back to him the whole while, then took the robe he held out and scurried into the bathroom without looking at him. "I can manage the rest myself," she said, not even looking back.

Sam told himself it was just as well. He breathed again, reminding himself that lusting after Josie was an exercise in frustration. He couldn't have her. He shouldn't want her.

He told himself to make his bed on the floor and be glad for it. He did. It worked until she came back.

The moment she walked across the room, stripped off her robe and climbed into the queen-size bed, only to look at him sweetly and say, "Thank you, Sam. For everything," all the desire he thought he'd tamped down rose strong and hard and aching once again.

He cleared his throat. "You don't have much to thank me for," he said hoarsely.

"For today," she said simply.

He shut his eyes. Today wasn't over yet.

It was, despite everything, one of the most memorable moments in Josie's life. Sam had stood up in front of his mother, a minister, friends and relatives, and had taken his vows with her. He'd given no indication that things weren't exactly what they seemed. Everyone undoubtedly thought they were snugly ensconced in the Captain's Quarters, wrapped in each other's arms.

No one knew the groom was sleeping on the floor.

Josie rolled onto her side now so that she could look at him. He was lying on his back, his arms folded under his head. She knew he wasn't asleep. She didn't know if he thought she was. Probably he hoped so.

She saw him flex his shoulders, then hunch them and roll over, nudging the floor, as if by doing so he could make it softer, more comfortable.

"Sam?"

He went totally still. She couldn't even see him breathing now. She edged closer to the side of the bed.

"Sam?"

"What?" Then suddenly he rolled to a sitting position and looked at her intently in the moonlight. "What's wrong? Are the contractions worse?"

Josie shook her head. "No. They've stopped. I..." She hesitated, then plunged on, "I wondered if you wanted to share the bed."

"*What?*"

She recoiled at the harshness in his voice. "I just thought...never mind," she said, turning away again, lying back down. Why had she thought he might? He wasn't drunk tonight.

She heard him get up and thought he was going to leave. Then she felt a hand on her shoulder. His touch was light, so light she thought for a moment she was imagining it. Then he curved his fingers and tugged so that she was forced to resist or turn to face him.

"You want...?" His voice trailed off. She saw him swallow. Was it that distasteful? she wondered.

"I said, never mind," she replied, her tone fierce. She turned away from him. But the next instant she felt the duvet jerked back and the bed sink slightly as Sam slid in beside her. He didn't just lie on his side, either. He spooned his body next to hers, so that they lay hard and warm together, the two of them.

Like lovers.

Josie felt his arm steal around her and she closed her hand over his, holding it fast against her belly. His breath came short and quick, stirring her hair, tickling her ear. She wriggled and the movement of her body rubbed his. And she felt him respond, felt the very obvious need in him press up against her.

It made her glad—and sad at the same time. It meant that his desire was not a one-time thing.

But the satisfaction of it would be.

"I can't—" she whispered, agonized. "The doctor said—"

"I know." His fingers tightened around hers. He pressed in more tightly still. His voice was aching, ragged. "I know."

"I can... I would... If you want... If you need..." Her voice faltered. Her cheeks warmed. She couldn't find the words to tell him what she would do for him if he wanted her to.

He turned his hand so that his fingers laced with hers. "It's all right. Go to sleep."

She looked at him wonderingly. "You're sure."

"I'm sure."

He was sure he'd die of frustration.

He was sure he had a terminal case of sexual excitement which constant exposure to Josie Nolan—no, Josie *Fletcher*—only made worse.

He should damned well stay away from her!

He couldn't do it.

Even after his relatives had scattered and his mother went back to New York and the guests returned in force, he couldn't go back to Coleman's Room and leave her alone in the library.

He told himself it was because he'd be too far away

if she needed something in the night. If she started having contractions for real, he would have to be there. He told himself it was because their guests would think it odd if they saw him coming out of Coleman's Room in the morning when it was clear that Josie was spending the nights in the library. Newly married couples didn't sleep two floors apart.

He told himself God would approve of him spending his nights with Josie—He would be glad Sam was suffering for his sins.

He was also, perversely, loving every minute of it.

He even stayed with her during the day. He went up to Coleman's Room to contend with whatever problems Elinor faxed or phoned his way from his New York office. But as soon as he could, he brought his portable phone or some paperwork downstairs so he could "keep an eye on Josie."

The same reasons applied, of course. How could she get ahold of him if she needed him?

"Buy a pager," Benjamin suggested.

"No," Sam said.

And that was that. Besides, he needed to make sure she didn't do too much. She was quite capable of thinking that she could do everything she'd done before she'd become pregnant. She still tried to do all the cleaning that she could on the main floor. And she would have tried to do the rest—and the laundry—if Sam hadn't insisted on hiring two high school students to come in and strip the beds, do the wash and remake up the rooms every day.

"How do I know they're doing a good job?" she complained the first day. "I can't even supervise them."

"I'll make sure they're doing it right."

"How do I know you'll know a good job?"

He looked down his nose at her. "I can tell a well-made bed as well as the next man."

Josie rolled her eyes. "Exactly what I'm afraid of."

"You've met my mother. Do you think she would tolerate less than hospital corners on every bed?"

"Well, all right." Josie gave in. Amelia's standards were nothing short of exacting. "But you have to check under the beds, too. No dust fuzzies. And make sure the towels are hung straight. And every room has fresh flowers. Two soaps. A lotion. A shampoo. A shoe-shining rag."

Sam made a list. He saluted.

She stuck her tongue out at him.

Then, when he was just about out of the room, she called after him, "What about your work? How can you spare time for mine? You have your own work to do."

"I'll manage."

"Can't I help you?"

He hesitated. But she looked at him so hopefully, so willingly, that he shrugged. "Maybe."

It was easier, he assured himself several times over the next week and a half, to let Josie do what she could to take some of the burden of his work while he did what she needed done in the inn.

He hadn't counted on her being quite so interested in the items he imported or the people who made them. Her questions were tentative at first, but became increasingly eager as he provided answers. He discovered how much he enjoyed sharing his enthusiasm for a particular artist or artisan. When he wasn't repainting the porch ceiling or sorting out guests or unplugging a sink, he drifted back to the library just to talk to her, to explain the whys and wherefores of the business and to regale her with stories about some of the craftspeople and artists he met during his trips.

It entertained her. It kept her from thinking about all the things she couldn't do since she was confined to the main floor of the house. It also pleased him. He liked seeing her eyes sparkle with enthusiasm. He liked the questions she asked, the quick curiosity she showed.

He caught himself about to say, *I could show you*, once when he was telling her about a Thai village he'd visited in pursuit of some particularly wonderful textiles. He didn't say it.

But, even though he swallowed the words, he wanted to take her there. And he wanted to show her the tiny shops in Hong Kong he frequented and the art dealer in Bali who kept his eye open for perfect pieces of art. He longed to be able to watch her face as she saw for the first time all the places that were common to him now.

But he wouldn't, because he would never take her there.

Theirs was a marriage of months, not years. Of convenience, not love. He was giving their child a name. He was giving Josie moral support at a difficult time. He was giving her a secure financial future.

He wasn't giving her forever.

It was just a matter of time, and she knew it. She had weeks with Sam. Months, maybe. That was all. She knew it.

She just wished her heart realized it, too.

It was easy to intellectualize, to tell herself that theirs wasn't a real marriage, that it would end in a matter of months or maybe even weeks, that there would come a time when Sam would be her child's father, but no longer her husband. It was even easy to believe it—in her mind. Not in her heart.

Her heart beat faster every time Sam came into the room. Her mouth smiled more often—every time, in fact, he slipped his arms around her in the dark of night. Her body grew soft and welcoming in the embrace of his. Even her mind began to betray her, to pretend that he loved her the way she couldn't stop loving him.

It was foolishness. Insanity. Impossible.

And yet she couldn't stop.

She asked herself why, if he didn't love her, he came to her every night and held her in his arms. She answered that he felt obliged to stay close so he could hear her call if she needed him to get her to the hospital. But he could have brought in a rollaway bed. He could have simply taken one cellular phone upstairs with him and told her to call him on the other one.

He could have. But he didn't.

He could have given her short answers to her questions about the objects he imported and the people who made them. He could have answered in monosyllables, instead of pulling up a chair and telling her tales of Singapore and Chiang Mai and Hokkaido and Bali.

He could have. But he didn't.

And so her heart began to sing. Her mouth continued to smile. Her mind began to hope.

If he didn't care for her, why had he got so upset that afternoon when he'd come downstairs from putting new glass in the skylight over Anna's Room to find Kurt in the kitchen drinking coffee with her.

He had stopped stock-still in the doorway, his normally cheerful greeting swallowed in the scowl that accompanied his sighting of Kurt.

"What the hell is he doing here?"

Josie, who had been smiling at one of Kurt's long-winded narratives about his flock, had blinked at Sam's ferocity. "Just visiting."

"I came to ask her to type a paper for me," Kurt said, always honest and forever, it seemed, oblivious.

"She can't."

Kurt stared at him. "But...she just said she would."

"She won't."

"But—"

Sam pointed at the paper sitting on the table in front of Josie. "Give it back to him," he said.

"It won't take me long," she protested. She had no desire to type the paper for Kurt. She hadn't seen him for a month—since the last time she'd typed something for him. She'd begun to realize she was well off without him. But there was something in Sam's tone, in the possessiveness of the way he was looking at her, that made her want to challenge him.

Or to understand him.

Was he jealous? Surely not. But then...

"Give it back." Sam said the words through his teeth. His fingers curled into fists at his sides. He looked strained and tired and sweaty and irritable. He looked as if he might take the top of Kurt's head off and enjoy it very much.

She picked up the paper and held it out to Kurt. "I'm sorry," she said. "I guess I won't have time right now."

Kurt looked from one to the other of them, clearly baffled by the dynamic between the usually unflappable Josie and the man she had married. "But you're just sitting around," he said, puzzled.

It was not the right thing to say.

Sam was halfway across the room before Josie got out

of her chair. She managed—just barely—to get between him and the still oblivious Kurt.

"I think there must be some work that Sam wants me to do," she said to Kurt. "You know, I told you I was working for him."

"Yes, but—"

"And it was lovely of you to drop by, but we ought to get started." She kept turning, keeping her face to Sam and her back to Kurt as Sam's path arced around her.

"I just got here," Kurt protested.

"Well, you can't stay." She was behind his chair now, doing her best to tug it out away from the table and send him on his way.

"Why not?"

Because if you value your life, you'll leave now. "Because Sam and I have work to do." She kicked Kurt's ankle.

"Ow." He bent to rub his ankle. Josie kicked his hand.

Finally he got the point. "Right. I, um, do have to be on my way." Scowling at her, he shoved his chair back and got up. He still had the paper in his hand and was looking at it as if trying to figure out how to leave it behind when he went.

"Don't forget your paper," Josie said firmly, herding him toward the door.

"No, don't," Sam said in a steely voice behind her.

Kurt looked from one to the other of them, then gave Josie what looked like one last hopeful smile. "See you soon?"

"Of course." She opened the door and practically shoved him through it.

Sam said, "Not on your life."

*   *   *

He had never wanted to take apart another man before.
Not piece by piece. He'd never wanted to blacken anyone's eyes or shove anyone's teeth down his throat.

Obviously there was a first time for everything.

And over what? Sam asked himself. It wasn't as if
he'd caught them in a compromising position. They'd
been in the kitchen, for heaven's sake! Fully clothed!
Josie had even been wearing an apron.

But she'd been going to type Kurt's paper. She'd been
going to let him back in her life. See him again. Talk to
him.

And then what?

They'd never know, Sam vowed. Because he wasn't
letting it get that far! Josie was, damn it all, *his* wife!

For now.

He stood on the edge of the bluff and jammed his
hands in his jeans pockets. He hunched his shoulders
and scowled out across the city. He rocked back on his
heels, then stared down at his feet and drew one deep
lungful of air after another.

"For now," he said aloud. "Just for now."

So what do you care what she does?

He didn't.

Did he?

Of course not. It was hardly a love-match. Not for
either of them. Josie didn't love him any more than he
loved her. It was just frustration that had had him jump-
ing down Kurt Masters's throat.

Sexual frustration.

He needed a woman.

He *had* a woman.

He had a *wife*.

That was the trouble.

CHAPTER NINE

SHE was the last person he'd expected to hear from when he picked up the phone that evening. "The Shields House," he said in his best innkeeper's voice.

"Sam?" He heard disbelief. Incredulity. Amazement. Followed by giggles. "Is that *you*?"

"*Izzy?*"

Another giggle. "*C'est moi.* How *are* you? I've been trying to call you for a week! Then I got brave and called your mother." Dramatic pause. "She told me you were in Dubuque."

"I'm in Dubuque," Sam verified. There was a pause. One second. Two. Three. He could almost hear the vibrations coming through the line, but he knew Izzy would wait forever before she said anything else.

So he said it for her. "I'm married."

"That's what she told me! How great! Oh, I'm so happy for you!"

No doubt she was. Knowing the extent of Izzy's ingenuousness, he was willing to bet she thought this was a love-match, that he and Josie had fallen as fast and as hard as she and Finn had.

"Finn didn't believe me when I told him," Izzy went on cheerfully. "Until I told him about the bab— Oops! I mean, well…" There was a typical Izzy pause for embarrassment. "Oh, Sam, I always say the wrong thing! I didn't mean to imply—"

"I know." Even though it was the truth and even though another woman would have. There wasn't a

146

spiteful bone in Izzy Rule's—no, Izzy *MacCauley's*—body. Sam knew that. All the same, he didn't want people saying he'd only married Josie because of the baby—even if it was true. "And now Finn believes it?" he asked dryly.

"Yes. I mean, is it? True? You are going to have a...?"

"It's true."

There was a moment's silence. Then Izzy said, awed, "You work very fast."

"It only takes once," Sam said, then could have bit his tongue off. It was no business of Izzy's how many times he'd taken Josie to bed! "So, what's up?"

"Well, I had a favor to ask. And it's really serendipitous, this favor...and you being in Dubuque and all. I couldn't believe it when your mother told me." The awkwardness was gone. She was Izzy again, talking fast and furious, expecting him to keep up and fill in the gaps for himself.

"What's serendipitous?" he asked her. "What favor? What about Dubuque?"

"Finn's looking for an inn."

"Finn wants to buy an inn?"

"Of course not. He needs to shoot a catalog at an inn—and environs. Sort of an Americana setting. Fourth of July. Bands and gazebos. That sort of thing."

"It's May."

"They work ahead," Izzy told him. "It's for a spring-summer collection next year. And he was trying to think of someplace different. They always do Puget Sound and Newport and Jackson Hole and places like that. So we were brainstorming last week, and I happened to remember your aunt's place in Dubuque."

"My place in Dubuque now," Sam said.

"Right. I was so sorry to hear about your aunt."

"Thanks. It's Josie's place, really," Sam qualified.

"That's your wife?"

He still hadn't got used to having one, and he hesitated a split second. Then, "Yes," he said firmly. "Yes."

"Well, do you suppose Josie would like to put us up for a week? They'd rent the whole place, give credit to the inn in the catalog. Feature it in some shots. It'd be great publicity. Great for tourism. Put Dubuque on the map."

"When did you go to PR school?" Sam grinned.

Izzy laughed. "You know me. When I think of a good idea, I go with it."

"Like Finn."

There was a jolt of silence. A long pause. Then, "Yes. Like Finn." Another pause. "You aren't angry about that, are you, Sam? You said you weren't. You sent him to me!"

He had. He hadn't wanted to, but Sam Fletcher always played fair. And he knew enough to know he didn't want to marry a woman who wanted someone else.

So he'd told Finn MacCauley a few home truths, then pointed him toward San Francisco.

"I know. I know." Sam rubbed a hand through his hair. "And no, I'm not angry. It's just that..." He sighed. "I don't know. You caught me by surprise, that's all."

"If you'd rather he didn't... Finn said you probably wouldn't want him there."

"No," Sam said quickly. "It's a good idea."

The more he thought about it, the better it was. "Be good for Josie. She could use some distraction. She's...

due in a month, and she's having a hard time. She has to take it easy.''

Izzy groaned. "Sam, having a houseful of guests is hardly easy.''

"Easier if they're the same people for a week," Sam said firmly. "And she won't shut the place down. Believe me, I've suggested it.''

"And she turned you down?" Izzy sounded amazed.

"You did," he reminded her.

"We're not going to talk about that anymore," Izzy said briskly. "Are you sure about this?''

"Yes. Like you say, it will be good for business. Put the place on the map.''

"All the better for when you sell it?''

His brows drew down. "What?''

"Well, I mean, you are, aren't you? Or *she* is. Josie. Your wife. You can hardly be going to move to Dubuque permanently," Izzy said impatiently.

Sam banged his forehead lightly against the doorjamb. "No. Of course not.''

He wouldn't be staying. But Josie would. He shut his eyes. "When does he want to come?''

"Sunday.''

He straightened abruptly. "As in two days from now?''

"Uh-huh. He'd have gone to Newport again if this hadn't worked out. This is so much better! So much fun. I'll get to see you, and meet your wife, and—''

"Whoa. Hang on. What do you mean, 'I'? You're coming, too?''

"Of course! And the girls, too." Finn's nieces, she meant. Pansy and Tansy. "We thought we'd take a little holiday—all of us together—the way we did when Finn took us to Jackson Hole. Only with better results," Izzy said a little wryly.

Sam remembered Jackson Hole. Izzy had come home and broken off their engagement. And left Sam in the lurch. Sam's mind began working overtime.

"Izzy, I don't know—"

"Oh, it will be fine," she assured him. "I promise. I'm so looking forward to meeting your wife. See you Sunday."

"Uh-huh," Sam mumbled into a dead phone. "I'm sure she'll look forward to meeting you, too."

Josie blinked back the tears that had threatened to spill over ever since Sam had told her the news.

Good news, he'd called it. *Good news?*

She should have known.

Isobel was coming. He hadn't got over her. Not at all.

A part of Josie was hurt. No. Devastated was closer to the mark. A part of her was furious.

How dared he bring the woman he loved—and had lost—to stay with them here! Did he expect to cavort with her under the noses of Isobel's husband and his own wife?

Probably. She could just imagine how appealing Isobel would be compared to his very pregnant wife. His very pregnant *unloved* wife! Josie swiped at the tears which had stopped threatening and actually spilled down her cheeks now. Damn Sam Fletcher anyway!

Well, fine. If that was the way he wanted things, so be it. She'd leave him to it. There was nothing to say she had to come out of the library at all. It would be just what the doctor ordered—this week of rest.

A week of rest! That was what he'd called it when he told her he'd agreed to having them come—Isobel and her photographer husband and whoever else was involved with this catalog shoot. He'd even dared to say he'd thought she'd be pleased.

Josie had said frostily, "How nice," and shut the door in his face. Locked it, too.

When he came to the library that evening, he had to knock, not just walk in.

She hadn't been going to let him in at all. She hadn't wanted him to see her bloodshot eyes or the tell-tale tracks of tears down her cheeks. In the end, she did, though, keeping the light off when she answered the door, then going back silently to get into bed.

"If you don't want them here," he told her, "I'll send them away."

And he'd probably go with them. She couldn't tell him to do that. Besides, she didn't want him thinking she was jealous, didn't want him knowing how much she cared.

"It's fine," she said tonelessly, and turned her back.

"You all right?" Sam asked as he slid in beside her and put his arms around her, drawing her close.

Josie swallowed, then nodded because she didn't trust her voice anymore.

But she wasn't all right. Not at all.

Josie had no trouble envisioning Isobel Rule. She was sure Sam's ex-fiancée would be tall and model-thin, with Audrey Hepburn cheekbones and a Mona Lisa smile.

So she had a hard time equating her vision with the reality of the short, bouncy young woman who threw her arms around Sam and gave him a hug, then turned to Josie and beamed.

"So you're the lucky lady," she said, giving Josie a hug, too. "I'm Izzy. I'm so glad to meet you."

Izzy.

Josie had heard Sam call her that, but she'd always thought of it as a sort of pet name that a fiancé would use. Now she saw that the name fit. Izzy didn't look like an Isobel. She wasn't tall, she wasn't reed-slender, and if there were cheekbones beneath those cheeks, Josie doubted they'd been seen in years.

Seeing Isobel should have made things better. Knowing that, even if she herself looked like a cow, Izzy was no *femme fatale*, either, should have improved Josie's mood.

It didn't—because Izzy was so obviously wonderful.

She was funny, she was sweet, she was thoughtful, she was kind. She charmed all the crazy technicians, hairstylists, wardrobe personnel and models. She doted on her little nieces. She was clearly in love with her dark, intense husband. And yet she seemed also to have a soft spot for Sam.

Izzy even—and this troubled Josie even more— seemed to want to be friends with her!

"Come sit by me," Izzy said when Josie appeared on the porch Sunday evening. She had just been going to check and see where Sam was—and hoped that Izzy was nowhere in the vicinity—when Izzy beamed up at her from the porch swing and beckoned.

"I can't," Josie said, backing away. "I have work to do."

"No work," Izzy said firmly, patting a spot on the swing. "Sam says no work. He says I'm supposed to distract you from work. That's what we're here for. To entertain you." She grinned.

"What?"

"Sit," Izzy commanded. "Sam says," she added firmly, as if there would be no discussion after that.

"Sam doesn't run my life," Josie muttered. But she came out and let the screen door bang behind her.

"No," Izzy agreed, but still she moved over to give Josie room to sit next to her. "He's much too nice."

"He's not nice!"

Now it was Izzy's turn to goggle. "He's not?" She looked genuinely surprised. "Sam?"

"He's a bully," Josie said truculently. But she came and sat down next to Izzy. She was cranky. Her back hurt and the baby was using her as a punching bag. It felt good to sit down. She shoved her hair back away from her face and wished she looked as cool and composed as Izzy.

The other woman tilted her head and smiled a little at her. "A bully," she said conversationally.

It wasn't precisely a question, but Josie answered her anyway. "Yes."

She stared straight ahead. She could see Finn and Izzy's little red-headed twin nieces playing catch on the front lawn. They had commandeered Finn and Sam into playing with them. Reluctantly Josie watched. Finn was certainly the more striking of the two men. He looked piratical even when he laughed. But Sam—

"Sam doesn't look like a bully," Izzy said softly.

No, he didn't. The wind was ruffling his sun-streaked hair. His shirttails were flapping in the breeze. He was laughing, too, as he stretched desperately to catch a wild throw by one of the girls. He made the catch and flipped the ball back to her, still grinning. Then when she deliberately threw it high and wide again, instead of throwing it back after he caught it, he made a growling noise and ran at her.

She laughed and ran, shrieking as Sam picked her up and swung her around, making her giggle.

"Now me!" the other twin cried, clamoring at him. "Swing me!"

Finn picked her up and swung her. Then, as Josie watched, the two men rearranged the twins so that each had a girl on his shoulders. One had her fingers tangled in Finn's hair, hanging on. The other gripped Sam's ears. They were all laughing.

No, Sam didn't look like a bully, Josie thought, swallowing against the painful lump in her throat.

He looked like a father.

"I like your wife," Izzy said to Sam.

They were sitting on the porch swing in the dark.

Finn was in the parlor going over some ideas with the catalog company rep. The models were wowing the locals down at the riverboat casino or one of Dubuque's more scenic nightspots. The twins were asleep.

Josie, too, had gone to bed early. Sam had hoped she'd come and sit with them on the porch and get to know Izzy. But shortly after dinner she had pleaded tiredness and retired to the library. He glanced over his shoulder now, through the window toward the library door. It was shut tight.

He looked down at his hands. "I like her, too."

"Of course you do," Izzy said with a light laugh. "You married her." She smiled at him.

He didn't quite smile back.

Izzy rocked them gently in the swing. "It's why I had to come," she said.

Frowning, Sam turned to look at her. "What's why?"

"I had to make sure you were happy." She gave a little satisfied bounce. "You are."

He looked at her. "How can you tell?"

"I've only got to look at you."

He looked happy? Sam was amazed.

"You're nervous," Izzy told him. "This is all new to you. And obviously you jumped the gun a bit. So you've got a bit of getting used to it to do."

"Oh, yeah," Sam said, deadpan.

"I'm not being critical. Finn wasn't exactly…reticent when it came to, um, bed." He could hear the blush in her voice.

A few months ago hearing about Finn's eagerness to take Izzy to bed would have annoyed the hell out of him. Now he was indifferent. He shrugged.

Izzy smiled. She reached out and patted his knee. "So…it all worked out, didn't it? My marrying Finn and you marrying your Josie."

"I don't know as I'd call her 'my' Josie."

"Of course she is." There was clearly no doubt in Izzy's mind. But then Izzy saw the world in black and white. She would never tolerate the muddled gray mess Sam seemed to be making of it.

Suddenly he couldn't sit here and talk about it anymore. He didn't feel right talking to Izzy about his marriage. The only person he should be talking to was Josie.

Not that he could talk to her. But he could be in bed with her.

Who knew how many more nights he would have?

He got to his feet and stretched his arms over his head, then dropped them and rocked back on his heels. Slowly and deliberately he yawned. "I'm pretty tired. Guess I'll turn in."

Izzy looked up at him and smiled. "Do that."

Her smile broadened and she looked up to see Finn coming out to look for her. She pushed herself up out of the swing and reached out to take his hands and look deeply into her husband's eyes. "I think I will, too."

*   *   *

She wondered if he was wishing he was in bed with Izzy.

He'd come in quietly and far sooner than she'd thought he would. She had already turned off the light and was lying in bed. But she wasn't asleep. She was thinking how nice Izzy was and how much she wished she could dislike Sam's ex-fiancée, but she couldn't. On the other hand, she couldn't sit out on the porch with them and make small talk, either.

It was beyond her tonight.

Let Sam do it. Let him eat his heart out if he had to. She just didn't want to be there to watch.

But the light hadn't been out more than fifteen minutes before the door opened and he came in.

She heard him move around quietly. She half wondered if he might be getting his things and leaving again. Not to try to sleep with Izzy. She knew very well that Izzy was in love with her husband.

But just so he didn't have to sleep with her.

He didn't leave again. He went into the bathroom. She heard the water running, heard him brushing his teeth. And then he was back—and slipping into bed beside her.

She didn't move. Held herself absolutely still. Barely breathed. Waited for him to roll on his side away from her and go to sleep.

He didn't move, either. Not at first. Then he rolled over, but toward her, not away from her. His arm went around her, curving close to her belly. He brushed his hand over its roundness in a gesture that felt almost possessive. Then slowly he drew her back against him into the warmth of his body. For an instant Josie tensed, resisted...gave in.

She wanted this. She wanted *him*.

A tear slid across her nose and fell onto the pillow. She closed her eyes and prayed no more would fall.

A steady drawing ache across her lower back woke her.

Nothing intense. Just…there. The ache had been a part of her so long that she couldn't remember when it had stopped feeling normal and begun to be something more. She turned a little, still caught in Sam's embrace.

He didn't wake as she shifted in his arms, but he turned, too, accommodating her. In the moonlight that cascaded through the window she watched him sleep, his firm mouth gentle now, lips slightly parted.

He looked beautiful. Silvery. Perfect. A corner of her mouth lifted. He didn't even snore.

The ache persisted, tightening a bit more as she lay looking at him. The baby stirred in her womb, pushing back.

She felt sometimes as if she was an unlucky bystander dragged into the battle for her body between her child and the organs it was pushing around. She tried to shift again, as if doing so would give one or the other of them more room.

It didn't.

She moved again.

Sam's eyes flicked open. "What's up?" His voice was soft and slightly gravelly.

Josie loved to listen to him when he first woke up. She loved to look at him then, too. For an instant he would look at her, unguarded and vulnerable, and she would wish he looked at her like that all the time. And then he would remember who he was—who *she* was— and the wall between them would fall back into place.

Her teeth closed lightly on her lower lip. "I think I may be having the baby."

*   *   *

He thought he was going to faint.

Last time he'd coped just fine. He'd bustled her off to the hospital, had been a tower of strength and fortitude.

This time, lying there in bed, flat on his back, hearing the words "...I may be having the baby" was enough to rattle him. He started to sit up and ended up lying back down again. He took a deep breath, then another, and another, while Josie watched him with wide, astonished eyes.

He felt like an idiot. He struggled to sit up and made it this time. "I'm sorry," he muttered. "It's just that—just that—" He looked at her closely. "This is it?"

She swallowed and nodded. "Uh-huh."

For her, he supposed, it would be a relief. She'd get her body back. For him—hell, he was going to be a father! Not at some indeterminate future time. But soon. Imminently.

In a matter of hours!

"Right." He got up to pull on his jeans. He fumbled, stumbled, almost fell on top of her. His hands shook. "I'm not prepared," he muttered. "Weren't we supposed to take breathing classes or something?"

"I did," Josie told him. "Before you got here."

Sam got his jeans zipped. "Good. Then one of us knows what she's doing. You can coach me."

Josie smiled.

He didn't realize how badly he needed to see her smile until that moment. He didn't realize how much he loved her until that moment.

Loved her?

Did he?

God help him, yes, he did.

It wasn't the bolt from the blue sort of love he'd once

imagined he would feel. It wasn't the spontaneous *yes* he'd felt when he'd fallen for Izzy. But it was deeper than either, stronger than both.

It was a love born not of the moment, but of a hundred—a thousand—tiny moments. He remembered them all—Josie as a teenager, fresh-faced and eager, quiet and watchful. Josie as a young woman, sweet and helpful. Josie swimming. Josie cleaning. Josie reading. Josie laughing. Josie touching.

Josie loving.

Loving him.

He wished to God he could remember more of that. He wanted desperately to remember it, wanted to know it, to feel it again. And again and again.

He saw her wince now and press a hand against her back. He dragged his mind out of the clouds and back to his wife, sitting on the bed before him. He wanted to tell her. He wanted to say, *I love you.*

He was afraid.

He was afraid she wouldn't want to hear it. It wasn't what he'd promised her when he'd married her. It was never a part of their bargain.

So he kept his mouth shut and held out his hand. "Come on. Let's go get this baby born."

CHAPTER TEN

YOU could always depend on Sam.

Josie knew that. She wasn't disappointed now.

All those stories about men falling apart when their wives went into labor were just so much nonsense when it came to Sam. He was so calm, so organized. So responsible. Just as she knew he would be.

He tried to pretend he was nervous. He even made her smile about her coaching him. But then, of course, he took charge.

He packed her bag. He called Benjamin and Cletus and made sure they would cover for breakfast in the morning. He woke Izzy and Finn, not even bothering to be circumspect about going up and banging on their door.

Moments later, Izzy, looking rumpled and well-loved, came down to see if there was anything she could do.

Josie glanced at Sam to see if he noticed the flush on Izzy's cheeks, but he barely looked at her. He just said, "Take care of things," and bustled Josie out the door.

Mr. Tact.

Well, maybe not. He didn't win any points for tactfulness at the hospital.

While they took Josie up to the obstetrics floor Sam did the paperwork in Admitting. By the time he got to the OB floor, she was in the birthing suite, and a nurse standing by the door barred his way in.

"You haven't attended prenatal classes," she told him. "They're a prerequisite."

"What my wife wants is the only prerequisite that matters," Sam replied bluntly. He looked past the nurse at Josie. "Do you want me?"

She knew he didn't mean it the way it sounded, the way she wanted him to. She knew he was only talking about the moment. She nodded. "I do."

It felt like taking a vow all over again.

He looked almost startled at her words. Then he nodded, too.

"Out of my way," he said to the nurse, and, if she hadn't moved, Josie was sure he'd have knocked her down.

Having a baby was a normal, natural event. Intellectually Sam knew that.

He knew that Josie was going through what millions of other women had gone through before her. He knew she was strong and healthy and that the sweat that broke out on her face and the strain he could see in every muscle of her body weren't anything to worry about.

He worried anyway. He couldn't help it.

And he couldn't help thinking it was all his fault.

If he hadn't— If he'd thought—

He bathed her face with a cool cloth. He rubbed her back and kneaded her shoulders. He tried to breath slow and deep to pace her, the way she told him the doctor had said he ought to do. It was the least he could do.

He wanted to say, *I'm sorry. I'm sorry.*

Whoever said women were the weaker sex had never seen one go through childbirth. He marveled at her patience. He marveled at her strength. Once more he wondered how tolerant he would be of giving control to a force outside his own will the way Josie was. Of course she had no choice.

But the grace with which she gave herself to the process inspired a respect in him that only heightened the love he felt.

She was stronger than he was. Braver than he was. He told himself he would have spared her if he could.

Yet at the same time he wondered if that was entirely true.

If he could have spared her this, he wouldn't be sharing it with her. He wouldn't be marveling at her, learning the depth of his love for her.

He wouldn't know the satisfaction of having her look at him for support when the doctor said, "All right. Let's get this baby born."

He wouldn't feel her death grip on his hands when the doctor told her to push.

He wouldn't hear her exclaim, "Look! Oh, look. Isn't he beautiful?" when their son came, red and squalling, into the world.

"Isn't he?" she demanded again in a tear-choked voice when he didn't answer at once.

Sam looked from the child to the woman who had borne him, tears mingling with perspiration on her face. He felt a tear or two of his own brim up. He didn't bother to blink them away. "Beautiful," he said huskily.

Not just the child. You.

Josie told herself it was worth it. It was nothing but the truth.

She wouldn't have missed it for anything—having this baby—this wonderful child named James Samuel Nolan Fletcher, but whom they called Jake. He was a good baby.

"The best," his father had said firmly.

But then, Sam would think that. He was already a doting dad.

He'd been a wonderful husband, too, all during the delivery. He'd been right there for her the whole time.

It was only afterward that he disappeared.

Josie had dozed off not long after the baby had slept, and when she awakened Sam was gone. She looked around the room for him, but he wasn't there.

The joy she'd felt, the euphoria that came with giving birth, evaporated. She felt lonely, abandoned, bereft.

Sam was gone. Just like that. It seemed like an omen, somehow, a portent for the rest of her life.

He'd come, he'd helped, he'd left.

She looked around the room again. There wasn't a sign of Sam's presence. Not a hint that he'd ever been in her life.

Except for Jake.

That was the way it would be soon enough, Josie knew. The adrenaline of childbirth was gone, too, now. Reality set in.

And the reality was this: Sam had married her to give his child a name; he had stayed around during her pregnancy to offer her his strength, his responsibility, his moral support; he had promised her the inn; he had guaranteed her financial security.

But then he would leave.

She'd always known he would leave.

They'd agreed on it. And then there would be just she and Jake.

So get used to it, she told herself, blinking back sudden tears. *Get used to it.* She sniffled and wiped at her eyes with the back of her hand. Be grateful for what you have.

She would. She swore she would.

But, God, did reality have to start so soon?

Had she been terribly foolish these past few weeks, letting Sam so far into her life—into her bed? Would it be worse now? she wondered. Was having had a taste of paradise worse than never knowing it at all?

They brought Jake home when he was two days old, arriving in the middle of a photo shoot on the front lawn. When they drove up, Josie saw baffles and lights and electrical cords, cameras and clothes, models and technicians and red-headed twins everywhere.

"I'll get rid of them," Sam offered.

"No. They're no problem." They'd be a distraction, and maybe a responsibility. And if Sam dealt with them summarily, it would be that much sooner that he'd be gone.

"But—"

"No!" she said sharply. "We can't throw them out," she added in a more conciliatory tone. "It wouldn't be good for the inn."

And that was something else she had to think about. Even if he agreed to keep her financially secure, it wouldn't be enough. She needed the inn to care about, to think about, to plan for.

She would need it more than ever after he was gone.

At her words, though, Sam gave her a hard look. Before he could say anything, however, Izzy and the girls came running up to see Jake.

They oohed and aahed and fussed over the baby and Josie, and all the while they did Sam kept moving Josie until he got her as far as the porch where she sat on the swing with the baby in her arms.

Izzy perched on the railing with a twin on either side of her. Three of the women models and the make-up artist came over and fussed over the baby, too. Even Finn and a couple of the men seemed to feel obliged to saunter over and give a thumbs-up. Josie was glad to have them all.

Sam gritted his teeth, looking as if he wanted to throw them out. But he didn't suggest getting rid of them again. Still, he did propose that she go into the library to rest.

"No," Josie said.

She didn't want to rest. She didn't want to be alone.

She knew what she would do if she were: think about the future she would spend alone. There would be time enough for that. She would have years to contemplate the barrenness of her life without Sam.

She turned away from him, grateful that Finn asked her something just then that she could answer. He stepped back and snapped her picture.

"Oh, heavens," Josie said, putting a hand over her face. "Not me! Not now."

"Don't worry," Finn said easily, still shooting. "I won't be putting them in any national magazines. It's just that I'm beginning to notice how motherhood makes beauties of you all." He turned then and shot a quick frame of Izzy, who blushed.

"Is that an announcement?"

Still red, Izzy nodded, and Finn looked at his wife with a love so tender it made Josie want to cry.

Please God, why couldn't Sam feel that way about her?

He was standing right next to the swing. If she turned her gaze slightly she could see his khaki pants-leg, see the impatient tap of his foot.

She could feel him staring down at her.

She couldn't return his gaze.

*   *   *

Somewhere along the line, he'd lost her.

Or maybe the truth was, Sam reflected as he stood on the bluff overlooking the city and didn't see it at all, he'd never really had her in the first place.

She had only married him because he'd made her pregnant. Not because she loved him. She'd married him because it was the right thing to do. Not because she wanted to spend the rest of her life with him.

She'd married him because he'd demanded it. That was all.

So why should he be surprised when she shut him out? Why should he feel hurt when she withdrew and her expression became shuttered?

He'd sensed that withdrawal almost at once—when he'd come back into her room at the hospital after having gone down to the gift shop to buy her some flowers.

When he'd come back, he'd expected to find her still sleeping.

She'd been awake. She'd even smiled at him. But then she'd looked away. Even as she took the bouquet of daisies and baby's breath with a watery smile she'd barely looked at him.

She acted as if she didn't care if he lived or died.

The truth was, she really didn't care. To Josie he didn't matter. Not now.

Not any longer. He'd served his purpose. He'd given her his support through the rest of her pregnancy and delivery. He would continue to give her his financial backing and their child his name.

But she didn't need him anymore.

Maybe she never had.

Maybe he'd only wished—

He shoved the thought away. But he couldn't shove another thought away: that soon he would have to leave and let her get on with her life. He knew that. He'd promised her.

And he'd do it. He would.

But not right away.

He couldn't leave right away. She was still recovering. She could still use him for a while yet. A few days.

Weeks? He could hope.

The thought made him breathe a little easier.

She could feel him drawing away from her. Minute by minute. Hour by hour. Day by day. She expected she would look up and see him checking his watch sometime, so desperate did he seem to be on his way.

He didn't want to sleep with her anymore. It seemed to go unspoken that now she'd brought Jake home from the hospital and moved out of the library up to her own quarters, her interlude in bed with Sam was over.

That first night he came and stood in the doorway and watched her settle Jake for the night. But when she went to get back into bed, he didn't follow her into the room. Instead he stayed where he was. He looked at the baby, then at the floor, and finally—at last—at her.

"You all right?" he asked.

What was she supposed to say? No?

Did he expect she would beg him to stay with her? Hardly. And he wouldn't want her to.

She nodded. "I'm fine."

"Then I'll let you get some sleep." And he tucked his hands in his pockets, turned and went away.

She didn't sleep all night. She dozed. She tossed and turned. At the merest of Jake's whimpers, she was out of bed and picking him up, needing to cuddle him close, to nurse him and rock him. Because he needed to be fed, she told herself. Because he needed her.

But she knew she needed Jake's warmth as much as he needed hers.

She looked down at him, sucking eagerly, his dark eyes unfocused, and she knew—just knew—they'd look at her someday the way his father did. "Oh, Jake," she whispered. "What am I going to do?"

He gummed her and then yawned and slept. And finally Josie, too, dozed, still in the rocking chair, still holding him in her arms.

A knock on the door woke her. She blinked and straightened. It was light, but still early. The baby muttered in his sleep.

"Shh," she whispered to him. Then, "Who is it?"

The door opened. Sam stood in the doorway, looking as if he hadn't slept anymore than she had. "I thought maybe I'd give you a break. Did you sleep all right?"

"Fine," Josie lied.

She watched warily as he came across the room toward them. She wanted to reach out to him and take his hand. She wanted to say, *I missed you last night. I wish you'd been here holding me.* She dropped her gaze and kept on rocking.

Sam stopped next to her chair. "I didn't hear him cry."

"I picked him right up."

"Then you couldn't have been sleeping."

She looked up to see his gaze challenging hers. She shrugged. "I'm attuned to him, I guess."

"I guess." He hesitated. "Give him here. I'll put him back to bed for you."

Sam scooped the baby into his arms and cradled him awkwardly against his chest. Jake stirred and frowned. Sam looked at him warily. But when Jake's frown turned to a whimper, and Josie half expected he'd hand the baby back, instead Sam rearranged him, murmuring, "Shh," and pressing Jake against his shoulder while he rubbed a big hand rhythmically against the baby's back.

Josie remembered that hand on her back.

She shoved herself abruptly out of the chair. "Since you're going to take care of him, I'll just go take a shower."

The shower, though, did nothing to erase the memory. Nor did it assuage the need. She stayed under the water a long time, and when she came out, she felt just as distressed as when she went in.

More so, in fact, because when she looked in the cradle beside her bed, Jake wasn't there. She rushed into the hallway, practically knocking over Izzy.

"Whoa, there," Izzy said with a grin. "Where's the fire?"

"I can't find Jake. Sam was just going to put him down and—"

"Sam's got him."

"But he was sleeping."

"He still is." She took Josie's hand. "Come with me." Izzy led Josie downstairs to the parlor.

There, on the settee, was Sam, stretched out on his back, sound asleep. Jake was sleeping on his chest, his thumb in his mouth, his tiny bottom in the air.

Josie swallowed against the lump in her throat. She couldn't say a word.

"I always knew Sam would make a great dad," Izzy said. "That's one of the reasons I wanted to marry him."

"Why didn't you?" Josie barely whispered the words.

Izzy smiled. "Because what we had doesn't hold a candle to what I've got with Finn. Nor to what Sam has with you."

Josie opened her mouth to protest, but couldn't.

How could she explain why she and Sam were married to the woman whose wedding had caused it?

She smiled because Izzy seemed to be expecting it. But as she looked at her husband and her son all she could do was wish to God it were true.

How long could he kid himself? Sam wondered. How long could he pretend she needed him to hang around?

Not long.

Finn and Izzy and their entire entourage left at the end of the week. When they did, Josie jumped back into the innkeeping business with a vengeance.

The moment the rooms were empty, she was filling them up again. Obviously it was to be business as usual for her.

Still Sam postponed his departure. He knew from the way Josie looked at him that she wasn't happy about it. But she didn't say anything. So he stayed on.

It might have been easier to look as if he was needed if Jake hadn't been such an easy-going baby. If he'd cried all night or fussed all day, thereby exhausting his mother, Sam could have said, You need to rest. I'll take over for a while.

But Jake was a perfect baby. He slept a lot, he nursed a bit, and when he was awake he seemed content to simply take in his surroundings with wide, unfocused eyes and periodically to gurgle and coo. The moment he did cry, Josie snatched him up, cuddled him or nursed him, and went right on with what she was doing.

Sam was superfluous, and he knew it.

He prayed she'd say, *Stay.* He would have in a minute. He hoped she'd say, *I need you,* or, better yet, *I love you.* If she had, he'd have dug in for the duration.

But she didn't. She barely looked at him, much less

talked to him. It was obvious she wanted him out of her
life.

So when Elinor called and said drily, "Remember
me? Remember Fletcher's? Remember Mr. Rajchakit?
He needs you in Thailand. Now," Sam had no reason
not to go.

Josie was sitting across the room in the rocker with
Jake in her arms. She was chatting with a couple of
schoolteachers from Ann Arbor who had come for their
twenty-fifth wedding anniversary.

Just outside the window another couple sat on the
front porch swing and listened to the lowdown on
Dubuque history from Benjamin. Down the way, by the
fence overlooking the road, Cletus was cutting back the
dead peonies. Overhead Sam could hear a vacuum running, pushed by one of the students.

"I'm leaving," he interrupted Josie and the teachers.
The words fell like stones into the conversation. Words
dried up.

They all turned to look at him. He looked only at
Josie. Her face was devoid of expression.

"I have to go to Thailand. This afternoon."

"Thailand. This afternoon? Imagine that," the woman
schoolteacher said. "All the way from Dubuque! That's
what they must mean about living in a global village."

"That's what I tell my students." Her husband pushed
his glasses up on his nose. "Just last semester I said…"

Sam didn't listen. He was looking at Josie. At Jake.
At Josie again.

Say something, he said to her with his eyes. *Give me
a sign. A word. A look. Stop me.*

She didn't move. Didn't even rock. Just sat, motion-
less, like a stone.

"—getting smaller every day," the man said with satisfaction.

"Where in Thailand are you going?" his wife asked Sam eagerly.

"I was in Bangkok once," her husband said. "After Vietnam. Just before the monsoon season..."

Sam watched Josie. Waited, hoped. Prayed.

"Have you ever been to Thailand, dear?" the woman asked Josie.

The words seemed to take a moment to penetrate. "What?" Josie looked startled, confused. She blinked, then shook her head. "N-no," she said, and turned her gaze on the guest. "No, I haven't. I probably never will."

Jake developed colic.

Sam never knew.

Errol Flynn had kittens. He missed that, too.

Cletus missed the forsythia and sliced into his thumb with the pruning shears. Both of the students quit to go on vacation. Josie had to find others. She did, but it wasn't easy.

Not that Sam ever knew.

He called her from Thailand. The connection was terrible. It crackled and popped and the delay was so long that they talked over the top of each other—when they talked at all.

It was awkward. Miserable. Worse, Josie thought, than if he hadn't called at all.

He called her from New York when he got back. The connection was better. They didn't talk over each other. The pauses seemed to last for hours, though in fact they were probably only seconds.

"How's Jake?" he asked every time.

"Fine," Josie said, whether or not it was true. Of course generally it was true. He wasn't ill or anything, just colicky. Fussy.

"What's he doing?"

"Sleeping," she said. Or, "Nursing," if he was doing that. She never said, *Crying*.

If she did he might think she wasn't coping.

He seemed to think that anyway. "I could come if you need me," he said to her at one point.

"No. Oh, no."

Missing him was terrible, but having him there, seeing him day after day, watching him with Jake and not being able to touch him would be even worse.

There was a silence. Then, "Fine," he said shortly. "It's not like I don't have plenty of work to do."

They never asked about each other. Only Jake.

Because only Jake mattered.

Josie told herself that every day a thousand times, whenever she thought of Sam, whenever she missed him and wanted him. She told herself that at night as she curled her arms around her pillow and tried to sleep.

Only Jake mattered. It was a mantra, echoing in her head over and over.

But as long and as often as she said it, she knew it wasn't true.

Sam mattered, too.

He bumped into Izzy in Central Park. Literally.

He was walking home from work, staring at his feet, filling up the hours, keeping himself away from the phone. It was like a lifeline—connecting him once a day to the two people on earth who gave meaning to his life. But they didn't know it, and he couldn't tell them. He could only grab on for a few minutes, ask a few awk-

ward questions, listen to Josie's equally awkward answers, take what joy he could from it, and then let go.

He had three hours to kill until he could call again
this evening. He was counting the minutes when he ran
into Izzy, in-line skating with the girls.

"Ooof!"

He looked up at the body he'd connected with in time
to grab her before she went down. "Izzy! Are you
okay?"

He hadn't seen her since she and Finn and the girls
had left Dubuque a month ago. A decade ago. A lifetime
ago.

She clutched his arms to keep herself upright. "Sam!
Fancy meeting you here!" She beamed and gave him a
smacking kiss on the cheek, then pushed herself back
from him and frowned. "You look like hell."

"Thanks very much," he said. "Sorry I can't say the
same."

Izzy looked wonderful. There was a bloom about her.
A glow that seemed to go with impending motherhood,
even though Izzy was still barely showing. He remembered that glow very well. He'd seen it on Josie's face.

"You shouldn't be skating," he said. "You could get
hurt."

"I'm pretty well padded," Izzy replied "And I'll stop
when the doctor tells me to stop. Unless you've taken a
medical degree since I last saw you."

Sam scowled at her. The twins, having glanced back
and noticed that Izzy had stopped, now skated back and
surrounded him.

"Hi, Sam! Where's Jake? Where's Josie?"

"Yes," Izzy said, looking around. "Where are Josie
and Jake? When did you get back?"

"A couple of weeks ago." Sam didn't answer the other question. "How've you been?"

"Fine. I'm glad you're back, though. I've been feeling this funny fluttery feeling, though. I think it might be the baby," Izzy confided. "I want to compare notes with Josie."

Sam looked at the ground. He looked past Izzy's left ear. He rocked on his heels and scratched the back of his head.

"Josie's in Dubuque," he said.

"In Dubuque? Why? Didn't you sell the inn yet?"

"We aren't going to sell the inn." He still didn't look at her. He wished he'd never let Izzy and Finn come out there. It would be so much easier if he didn't have to explain.

"So is Josie training a new innkeeper?"

"No, Josie's not training a new innkeeper. Josie's staying there."

Izzy stared at him, her eyes widened, then narrowed. Her brows drew down. "What do you mean, staying there?"

"Just what I said. We're...not staying together."

"Why not?"

He scowled furiously. "Izzy! Damn it! You're not supposed to ask things like that!"

She slapped her hands on her hips. "I'd like to know why not! It seems a perfectly reasonable question given the fact that a month ago you two were inseparable."

"She was pregnant! She needed me then!"

"And now she doesn't?" Izzy said sarcastically.

Sam ground his teeth. "No, damn it, she doesn't."

"A woman with a brand-new baby, three cats, a dog, a couple of doddering old men and a twenty-room inn doesn't need any help?"

"Not from me," he said stubbornly.

"She told you that?"

"Yes." The word hissed through his teeth.

"I don't believe it." She paused, considering, then said almost musingly, "Maybe I do."

"What's that mean?"

Izzy cocked her head and looked at him. "Did you ever *once* tell her you loved her?"

Sam hunched his shoulders. He scuffed the toe of his loafer in the gravel on the pathway. He didn't answer. That, apparently, was answer enough.

Izzy groaned. "Sam," she said in long-suffering exasperation.

"She wouldn't want to hear it," he argued. "She didn't want to marry me! We got married because of Jake, damn it! I forced her to marry me."

"Figures," Izzy muttered under her breath. Then she looked at him. "But you didn't force her to make love with you when you got her pregnant, did you?"

Sam stared at her, aghast. "Of course not!"

"Well, then, why do you think she did it?"

He felt the flush creep up his neck. He didn't want to explain the circumstances of that evening to anyone— especially not to Izzy!

"We'd been drinking," he said. "It was a trying time for both of us. You— She— Kurt—" He couldn't articulate it. "It wasn't because she loves me!"

"Sam," Izzy said, disgusted, "just how big an idiot are you?"

CHAPTER ELEVEN

SAM FLETCHER had always had the courage of his convictions, the determination that came with knowing he was doing the right thing, making the smart move. When it came to his business dealings, he stepped boldly, willing to risk unflinchingly whatever was needed to get what he wanted.

So why couldn't he just pull up his socks and go straight out to Dubuque and confront Josie—*ask* Josie if she loved him, *tell* Josie that he loved her?

Why did he stall three days? A week? More? Still unable to make the move Izzy had told him he was crazy not to make.

"I can't believe you," she'd railed at him that afternoon in the park. "Are you blind? Josie is nuts about you!"

"No," he'd said. She wasn't.

Was she?

Did he dare start hoping again? He'd hoped before. He'd watched her every waking moment, it seemed, looking for clues—a word, a gesture, a smile.

He hadn't seen a thing.

Was that what he was still afraid of? But then, he asked himself, what would be worse than what he already had, which was nothing?

He was afraid she could tear out his heart.

Maybe—and this he hadn't told Izzy—it was because he'd been rejected once before.

He'd thought he was in love when he was engaged to

Izzy. He'd thought Izzy was in love with him. But what they'd had hadn't survived Finn's challenge. And though he'd let her go with a smile and a wave, the truth was he'd been hurt.

He knew how badly her rejection had hurt him. And that hurt didn't compare to what he would feel if Josie were to flat out tell him she didn't love him, never could love him.

If he didn't go, he could pretend. He could convince himself that she cared a little, might care more someday if he gave her space, time, and if he nurtured the notion of loving him carefully and let it grow on her. It could take years.

Sam had always thought he was a patient man. Hah. Still he didn't go. He called. Every night.

"How's Jake?" he asked her. *Do you love me?*

"Is he getting bigger?" *Do you miss me?*

"Does he smile yet?" *If I told you I love you, would you care?*

And every night he got her answers. But what he wanted were the answers to the questions he never dared voice.

Every night he hung up the phone lonelier and more bereft than the night before.

"I don't understand why Josie is staying in Dubuque?" his mother said every other day. She'd fix a frown on her son. "I don't understand why you're letting her?"

"Josie had a life before she married me," Sam replied. It wasn't an answer. But he couldn't find the guts to tell his mother the truth.

"You know," Elinor, his assistant, said conversationally one afternoon as she scraped into a pile the deskful of phone messages he'd never returned, "if I didn't doubt that cloning humans was a cottage industry in Dubuque, I'd swear they cloned a Sam Fletcher and sent the incompetent one back to New York."

Sam looked at her blankly. "What?"

"Let's just say you were more efficient when you were wallpapering with one hand and running the whole show on the phone long-distance with the other! Go on back to Dubuque, Sam. Go home to your son and your wife!"

He would, he thought as he dropped the mail on the kitchen counter of his Fifth Avenue penthouse apartment, if he thought for one minute that Josie wanted him the way he wanted her.

He sighed and idly spread the mail around, pushing the junk and the ads and the circulars into the trash. That left the bills. And—he frowned at the handwritten envelope addressed to him.

He picked it up and slit it open. A photo fell out. And a note. From Izzy. It had just one sentence written on it: "Finn says to tell you a picture is worth a thousand words."

He let the note flutter to the countertop. He stared at the picture in his hand. It was one of the ones Finn had taken the afternoon Sam had brought Josie and Jake home from the hospital. She was sitting on the porch swing holding the baby, but she wasn't looking at the baby. She was looking up at the man wearing the khaki trousers who stood beside her.

Sam knew the man—he *was* the man.

He remembered the moment. He'd been looking at Jake, wishing he dared look at Jake's mother, that he dared tell Jake's mother how much he loved her. But he hadn't.

Now he saw Jake's mother looking at him.

He never remembered having seen Josie looking at him that way before. He'd never caught that tender yearning in her eyes, had never dared imagine that look of longing on her face.

Was it real?

Or was Finn just a very good photographer?

Josie was elbow-deep in cream cheese, apples, cinnamon, raisins and praying that Jake wouldn't wake until she had finished mixing the filling for tomorrow's breakfast crepes. He'd been fussy all day.

"Teething," Benjamin had said.

"He's only six weeks old," Josie had pointed out.

But Benjamin had been adamant. He and Cletus doted on their "honorary grandson," and as far as they were concerned he was miles ahead of every other child his age—even when it came to making his mother miserable with his crying, apparently.

He had fallen asleep, at last, shortly after nine. Josie had been relieved because then Sam wouldn't hear him crying when he called.

He called every night—not always around nine, but generally within the hour. She'd had the cellular phone in her pocket while she ran up to remove a feather quilt that one of the guests had suddenly discovered she was allergic to, came back down to transfer Errol's kittens out of the butler's pantry, where the cat had carried them and put them back in the basement where they wouldn't be underfoot tomorrow.

She'd set the phone in the middle of the table while she'd laid out place settings for the fifteen guests who would be there tomorrow for breakfast. She'd lugged it with her while she went up to the third floor to deliver a late-arriving bouquet of flowers, and when she'd tracked down Cletus to go rescue a couple whose car had died in the parking lot of the riverboat casino.

By the time she got to the cream cheese and apples, she was worried that Jake might be stirring and start to cry again. But a quick check of him in his pram, tucked away in the butler's pantry where she could hear him while she worked, proved that he was, blessedly, still asleep.

So she dove into kneading the apples, cinnamon and raisins into the cream cheese and prayed that Jake wouldn't wake and Sam wouldn't call until she was done.

She had cream cheese all over her hands when she heard the first whimper. Then there was a sniffle. A sob.

Then a full-throated Mommy-where-are-you-I'm-hungry! cry.

"Damn!" She gave the cream cheese mixture one last squish and tried to scrape it off her hands. It globbed and plopped. Mostly it stuck.

"I'm coming, sweetie!" she crooned, grabbing up the bowl with her forearms and carrying it into the butler's pantry.

Jake howled on.

"I'm coming. Just hang on."

She turned to put the bowl down and ran smack into a hard, masculine chest.

"What's wrong with him?"

She opened her mouth and closed her mouth, word-less, gaping. *Sam?* Here?

He took the bowl out of her hands, set it on the counter. "What's wrong with him?" he demanded again, craning his neck to see past her toward the pram.

"H-he's hungry," Josie sputtered. "I've g-got to feed him."

"So wash your hands."

"I will. I am! What are you doing here?"

He didn't answer, just moved past her to pick up the baby. "God, he's grown! He's twice the size he was!"

Sam lifted Jake out of the pram and held the squalling child up to get a look at him.

"Hardly," Josie said, scrubbing furiously at her hands and glancing back at him. "What are you doing here?" she demanded again.

"Holding my son." Sam shifted Jake in his arms, cradling him against his shoulder, rubbing his back. Jake sniffled and hiccoughed and gummed his fist.

Josie found herself patting her pocket, checking for the phone—as if she might have left it somewhere and had somehow conjured Sam up in the flesh to take its place.

She turned around to find Sam had brought Jake into the kitchen and was waiting expectantly until she'd seated herself in the rocker. She did, then looked at him, but he didn't hand Jake over. He still waited.

Self-consciously she opened her blouse, then held out her hands for Jake, not looking at Sam at all.

There was a moment's pause. Then she heard the soft intake of Sam's breath, and he settled the baby in her arms.

Jake glommed on greedily. Josie held him protectively close, though who she was protecting wasn't too hard to guess.

Sam hunkered down next to the rocking chair.

She didn't look at him. Couldn't. "What?"

"I love you."

Her head snapped around. A girl could get whiplash hearing unexpected things like that!

Or maybe she hadn't heard it. Maybe she'd just dreamed it. She frowned.

"Don't." His voice was soft, and he reached out a hand and smoothed her brow.

If she'd had a free hand, she'd have batted his away. What was he trying to do to her?

"Don't what?" she said crossly, shaking her head, trying to escape his touch.

"Don't frown. Don't fight me." His voice dropped, gentled. His warm brown eyes melted her. "Don't tell me to go away."

She shook her head, confused. Desperate. It was like having your best dream turn into your worst nightmare. "What are you talking about?"

"Us."

"What us?"

"The us I want to be married for real." His gaze never left hers.

"You don't love me," she argued, afraid to hope.

"I do."

"You didn't!"

"I do now. I have for—hell, I don't know how long." He shook his head. "I'm not exactly quick on the uptake, I guess." He smiled ruefully. "I knew you were driving me nuts, but I didn't figure out it was love until your labor started."

"When my labor started? What happened then?"

"I wanted to make you smile."

It was so simple—and so illogical—that Josie couldn't doubt it. She laughed. She shook her head and blinked back a sudden surge of tears.

"Why didn't you say so?" she asked, her voice wobbling.

A corner of his mouth tipped. "I didn't think you loved me."

"But—"

"You certainly never said you did."

"I was supposed to? When you were pining over another woman?"

Sam grimaced. "Izzy told me I was an idiot."

"You talked to Izzy about it?"

"I didn't have to talk to Izzy," Sam said ruefully. "She talked to me."

"And you believed her?" Had it truly been that simple?

"I wanted to. I was afraid to. Then she sent me a picture."

He straightened up and dug his wallet out of his back pocket. He took out a photo and handed it to her.

Josie looked at it—at herself. She'd had no idea her feelings for Sam were so apparent. She'd had no notion at all that every ounce of love and longing she felt for him was there for the world to read on her face. She bent her head and studied Jake's soft hair. She touched his cheek. Sam's hand came out and took hold of hers.

"You love me." His whispered words weren't quite a question. They were, however, brimful of awe—and of hope.

Josie dared to raise her head and look at him. "I have," she said softly, "for years."

"Years?" Sam sounded indignant.

"Since the very first time I saw you—that summer when I was the cleaning girl. You were my idea of the perfect man."

He snorted and looked faintly embarrassed. "Hardly." His voice was gruff.

"I thought so," Josie said.

"You were going to marry Kurt."

"You were engaged to Izzy," she reminded him. "It was a mistake, getting engaged to Kurt. I know that now. I wasn't right for him."

"He wasn't right for you."

"Both," Josie agreed. She wasn't going to argue about it. "I hope I would have seen that before I did anything stupid." She twisted the corner of Jake's blanket around her fingers.

Sam hesitated. "You didn't think going to bed with me was stupid?"

"Oh, no." Josie shook her head. "Well," she admitted, "maybe from a self-preservation standpoint it was. But..." She looked into his eyes and hoped he could read in them the feelings she still hadn't found the words to say. "I'd do it over again," she told him. Her gaze dropped then and she smiled down at her son.

"For Jake."

Their eyes met. Slowly, Josie shook her head. "No. Not just for Jake. For you."

He moved in then, angling around so that he didn't mash Jake, still nursing between them, and he touched his lips to hers. Then, much too soon for Josie, he pulled back and fished another picture out of his wallet.

It was the one Finn had taken right after he'd taken the shot of Josie. In it Sam was looking down at his wife and son, and the expression on his face was a look identical to hers. Josie stared at it, then at her husband.

He smiled. "For you," he said. "So you'll never forget how much I love you, too."

"Do you think Hattie will care if you sell the inn?" Josie asked him much later that night—well, actually sometime early the next morning—as they curled together in her bed.

"I think that's exactly what Hattie had in mind when she left it to me," Sam said. "I think Hattie orchestrated this whole thing."

"What about the dog and the cats?"

"We could sell them, too."

"No!" Josie started to sit up, but he tugged her back down into the curve of his body and held her there. "We can't," she said. "They're family."

"All right. We'll keep them," Sam said. Well-loved and at peace with the world, he was amenable to almost anything right now.

"What about Benjamin and Cletus?"

"We're not keeping them!"

"But they'll be lonely."

"They can come and visit."

"They'll want to watch Jake grow up."

"We'll come and visit them," he promised.

Josie smiled. "Good. I want to come often. I'll miss them. I'll miss the inn. I'll miss Dubuque."

"We're not bringing Dubuque!"

She laughed. "I love you, Sam."

He rolled her in his arms and braced himself over her. "I love you, too."

"Show me?"

"Again?"

She traced the inner curve of his ear with her finger, sending a shiver along his spine. "Well," she said, smiling impishly, "if you'd rather not..."

He grinned down at her. "Oh, I'd rather, Mrs. Fletcher. In fact," he told her with considerable satisfaction as he began once more to love her, "I can't think of anything I'd rather do."

Coming Next Month

HARLEQUIN PRESENTS®

THE BEST HAS JUST GOTTEN BETTER!

#1935 LOVESTRUCK Charlotte Lamb
Nathalie's boss, Sam, was a little the worse for wear when he proposed to her at a party, so she decided to play along and pretend she believed he meant it. And soon she was really beginning to wish he *had*....

#1936 SCANDALOUS BRIDE Diana Hamilton
(Scandals!)
Nathan's whirlwind marriage was already heading for the rocks—he was sure his wife was having an affair with her boss! It seemed the only way to save the marriage was to learn the truth about his scandalous bride once and for all....

#1937 MISTRESS AND MOTHER Lynne Graham
Since separating on their wedding day, Molly maintained that nothing could persuade her to share her husband's bed.... Until Sholto agreed to settle her brother's debt—in return for the wedding night he never had!

#1938 THE LOVE-CHILD Kathryn Ross
(Nanny Wanted!)
When Cathy turned up at Pearce Tyrone's villa in the south of France, he assumed she was the nanny he'd been waiting for. But she knew it was only a matter of time before he found out that she wasn't all she seemed....

#1939 SECOND MARRIAGE Helen Brooks
(Husbands and Wives 2)
Claire would make the perfect bride—everyone said so. But Romano Bellini didn't want his life complicated by a second wife. Curious, then, that the subject of marriage just kept coming up!

#1940 THE VALENTINE AFFAIR! Mary Lyons
Alex had promised her newspaper a Valentine exclusive on Leo Hamilton. And after dogging Leo's all-too-attractive heels, she realized she wanted him as an exclusive, all right—exclusively hers!

**Look for these titles—
available at your favorite retail outlet!**

January 1998
Renegade Son by Lisa Jackson
Danielle Summers had problems: a rebellious child and unscrupulous enemies. In addition, her Montana ranch was slowly being sabotaged. And then there was Chase McEnroe—who admired her land and desired her body. But Danielle feared he would invade more than just her property—he'd trespass on her heart.

February 1998
The Heart's Yearning by Ginna Gray
Fourteen years ago Laura gave her baby up for adoption, and not one day had passed that she didn't think about him and agonize over her choice—so she finally followed her heart to Texas to see her child. But the plan to watch her son from afar doesn't quite happen that way, once the boy's sexy—*single*—father takes a decided interest in *her*.

March 1998
First Things Last by Dixie Browning
One look into Chandler Harrington's dark eyes and Belinda Massey could refuse the Virginia millionaire nothing. So how could the no-nonsense nanny believe the rumors that he had kidnapped his nephew—an adorable, healthy little boy who crawled as easily into her heart as he did into her lap?

**BORN IN THE USA: Love, marriage—
and the pursuit of family!**

Where were you when the storm blew in?

Snowbound

Three stormy stories about what happens to three snowbound couples, from three of your favorite authors:

SHOTGUN WEDDING by Charlotte Lamb

MURDER BY THE BOOK by Margaret St. George

ON A WING AND A PRAYER by Jackie Weger

Find out if cabin fever can melt the snow this December!

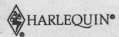